"Promise me you're one of the good guys," Lily said softly.

Brand went totally still. Lily waited, not breathing. A tremor of apprehension slid through her. Finally, to her relief, he spoke, but his words were not comforting.

"I can't promise you that. I don't feel like a good guy right now. I feel like a heel, allowing you to get so deeply involved. I should have been able to do something to help you."

"You saved my life." Tentatively she put a hand on his flat abdomen and felt the muscles quiver at her touch, felt him sigh in frustration.

"For now. There's going to be more danger and there's nothing I can do to avoid it. If I trust the wrong person, you could be facing a gun. But I *can* promise you that I will protect you with my life."

 HARLEQUIN®

992
May

INTRIGUE®

MALLORY KANE

JUROR
NO. 7

Recycling programs
for this product may
not exist in your area.

Copyright © 2008 by Harlequin Books S.A.

ISBN-13: 978-0-373-15088-5
ISBN-10:   0-373-15088-1

The contents of this book may have been edited from their
original format. The publisher acknowledges the copyright
holders of the individual works as follows:

JUROR NO. 7
Copyright © 2007 by Rickey R. Mallory

Excerpt from SECRETS IN FOUR CORNERS by Debra Webb
Copyright © 2009 by Harlequin Books S.A.

This edition published by arrangement with Harlequin Books S.A.

® and TM are trademarks of the publisher. Trademarks indicated with
® are registered in the United States Patent and Trademark Office, the
Canadian Trade Marks Office and in other countries.

www.eHarlequin.com

Printed in U.S.A.

ABOUT THE AUTHOR

Harlequin Intrigue author Mallory Kane has always loved reading and writing stories. She credits her love of books to her mother, a librarian, who taught her that books are a precious resource and should be treated with loving respect. Her father and grandfather were steeped in the Southern tradition of oral history, and could hold an audience spellbound for hours with their storytelling skills. Mallory aspires to be as good a storyteller as her father. With fifteen books to her credit, she's well on her way. When she's not writing, Mallory creates and designs greeting cards. She lives in Mississippi with her husband and their two cats.

For more information about Mallory visit her Web site at www.mallorykane.com or send an e-mail to mallory@mallorykane.com.

CAST OF CHARACTERS

Lily Raines—Targeted by the mob to deadlock a jury and let a murderer go free, Lily finds herself on the run with the ruggedly handsome enforcer who threatened her.

Brand Gallagher—The brave undercover cop is forced to terrorize lovely juror Lily Raines. When she's targeted for death, he knows one of his fellow officers has betrayed him. Can he stay alive long enough to get Lily to safety and expose the traitor?

Giovanni Castellano—When the crime boss's number one hit man is indicted for murder, he swears revenge. He will free his soldier, and woe to any innocents who get in his way.

Armand Foshee—The sadistic Cajun would have killed Lily if Brand hadn't stopped him.

Thomas Pruitt—Brand's new boss is tough and ambitious. But he's lied to Brand at every turn. How far will Pruitt go to further his own career?

Gary Morrison—His former lieutenant has always been the one man Brand could trust. Suddenly the things he tells Brand don't add up.

Al Springer—Brand's fellow undercover officer has a spotless record. But has he finally crossed the line?

Leroy Carson—The third undercover cop infiltrating Castellano's operation, Carson has always been a good cop, but is it just an act?

Chapter One

Something was wrong. Lily Raines knew it as soon as the door closed behind her. It was too dark, the only light coming from the streetlamp outside her living room window. Hadn't she left the light on over her sink? She set down her purse and keys and listened.

Nothing.

The light must have burned out. She puffed her cheeks in a weary sigh and shrugged out of her jacket, the rustle of silk echoing in the silence.

Her scalp tingled with that creepy spider-on-your-skin feeling—as if someone were watching her. She'd had it ever since the trial started.

Stress. That's all it was. Goodness knew she had enough reason.

She reached for the living room light switch.

"I wouldn't do that."

Lily shrieked.

A dark figure rose up in front of her.

She tried to scream but her throat seized, tried to turn and run but her legs wouldn't carry her.

Hard hands grabbed her shoulders, twisted her violently and shoved her onto the couch.

Gasping for air, Lily bounced back up and swung her fist at the dark shape. She connected with flesh.

"Ouch! *Maudit!*" The owner of the voice grabbed her and shoved her again, hard. She fell across the arm of the couch and onto the floor, bumping her hip and elbow painfully.

"Hey—"

Different voice. There were two of them. Panic clawed at her throat and she scrambled to regain her footing. She screamed for help and tried to get up but her head hit the end table and she saw stars. She tried to crawl away but there was nowhere to go. They were between her and the door.

"Get her!"

A different pair of hands closed around her upper arms from behind and lifted her with no effort.

"Let go of me!" she cried, kicking backward. The hands turned into steely arms that wrapped around her, immobilizing her. This one was big, tall, solid. His breath sawed in her ear.

She stomped but missed his instep. His hold tightened. She clawed at his forearms, but he squeezed her so fiercely she could barely breathe. She gasped for air.

The first man stepped in front of her and into the faint light from the window. She squinted. He was skinny. Her height, maybe. Shorter than the one who held her. She'd need that information later to tell the police—if they let her live.

Desperately she kicked, using the second man's hold for leverage. He squeezed her until her ribs ached and whispered something close to her ear. She didn't understand what he said, but the feel of his hot breath on her skin sent terror streaking through her.

The skinny guy laughed as he dodged her kicks. Then his laughter stopped and he grabbed her chin. He stuck his face in front of hers. His breath reeked of garlic. "Calm yo-self, *Lily*."

He knew her name? She froze, horrified. These men weren't burglars. This was personal.

"Who are y—"

The fingers moved from her chin to her throat. "Good girl. Now you gon' be quiet for me?"

His fingers pushed painfully into her neck as she tried to nod. Tried to stop her brain from imagining what they planned to do to her.

Frantically, she searched her memory. She didn't recognize the voice or the accent. Cajun, maybe. She'd never done anything to anybody.

"What do you want?" she gasped.

The Cajun bared his teeth and his fingers tightened. Her larynx closed up. He was crushing it. He was going to kill her.

"Di'n I tell you be quiet?"

She struggled for air. She didn't want to die. She made a strangled sound and clawed at the arms holding her. Her vision went black.

"Careful," the man who held her rasped. "She can't breathe." The punishing pressure on her chest relaxed slightly.

"You shut your face!" the skinny guy hissed, but he loosened his hold.

She sucked air through her aching throat. From behind her the rock-hard arms loosened a bit more.

Her eyes were beginning to adapt to the darkness, but she still couldn't distinguish features or clothing. There was too little light and she was too afraid. She swallowed, her throat moving against the Cajun's hand.

"Just tell me what you want. I don't have much money—"

He released her throat and snagged a handful of her hair, twisting roughly.

Tears of pain sprang to her eyes.

From somewhere he pulled out a long, thin-bladed knife. He held it up before her eyes, then touched its point just beneath her chin.

"Come on, *Lily,* don't make me hurt you. I will, and I'll enjoy it."

The man holding her tensed up. His forearms, strapped under her breasts, tightened.

She strained backward as far as she could. The Cajun grinned at her fear. She swallowed and felt the point of the knife prick her skin. Between the hand clutching her hair, the knife and the other man holding her, she was totally helpless. Totally at the mercy of merciless men. They could do anything to her.

"Understand?"

She nodded jerkily. Tears slid down her cheeks. They were going to kill her and she didn't even know why.

"You're on the jury for Sack Simon's murder case."

She stiffened in surprise. *The trial!* Her pulse thrummed in her ears.

"Aren't you?"

"Yes," she whispered. Her fists clenched automatically and her fingernails dug into the arms holding her.

"My boss, he wants the trial over. He don' want Simon convicted."

Lily stared at the shadows of his face. Sharp chin. Long nose. Eyes that were nothing but black holes.

"I—don't understand." She didn't. The trial was half over. The prosecution had presented ample evidence to put Simon away for life.

"Den I make it simple, *Lily*. The jury can't convict Simon."

The way he kept saying her name terrified her.

"Can't convict—?" she repeated, trying to make sense of what he was saying. Her brain wouldn't work. How could they not convict? "But he's guilty."

The Cajun pressed the knife blade harder, just enough to sting her neck. "Damn it, woman. I know you ain't that stupid. 'Cause if you are, I might as well just kill you now."

Suddenly, she got it. They wanted her to hang the jury. "But I can't—"

He let go of her hair and grabbed her throat again, squeezing.

She coughed.

"Pay attention, Lily. The only thing you can't do is tell anyone we was here. My boss wants to know that *you* will vote not guilty."

"Not guilty? That won't work. There's too much evidence. There's DNA."

"Shut up." He tightened his hold on her throat.

She gagged and lost her footing as the man holding her pulled her away from the little guy's punishing grip.

"Stop choking her," he snapped.

"Hey, *bioque*. You don' give the orders. I do." The skinny Cajun turned his attention back to Lily. He grabbed her jaw again.

"Evidence can be wrong. Do you understand, *Lily?*"

One juror out of twelve. A hung jury. They wanted her to force a mistrial. She nodded.

"Tell me!"

"You want me to vote not guilty." She coughed again, her throat raw and sore.

"You understand why?"

"To deadlock the jury. A mistrial," she croaked.

"Good girl." He patted her cheek. His fingers smelled of garlic and cigarettes—a sickly, stomach-churning mixture.

By contrast, she had a vague sense of soap and mint from the man behind her. He'd bathed and brushed his teeth before coming here to terrorize her? The thought nauseated her.

The garlicky fingers slid down her neck and past the vee of her shirt to touch the top of her breast in an obscene caress.

Lily's stomach turned over. She recoiled, straining backward against the other man. "Please—please don't hurt me."

The man holding her backed up enough to pull her away from the Cajun's probing fingers.

Of the two of them, she'd rather be at the mercy of the bigger man. He seemed to be trying to keep her safe from the little Cajun's pawing.

"Wh-why me?" she stammered, turning her head away from the man's leering gaze.

"My boss, he's a very smart man. He studied the jury. Then he picked you. You the perfect juror."

She didn't have to ask why. She knew. It was because she lived alone and her interior design business was at a virtual standstill since her biggest client had declared bankruptcy. She'd cleared her schedule to design the interior of their high-rise and now she was out of a job.

There were eight men and four women on the jury. The other women had children, husbands, jobs. The attorneys had asked each one about family.

Family.

"Oh, God." Her eyes widened in horror as the real reason she'd been chosen dawned on her. *Her father.* He was in a nursing home, helpless to defend himself. They could hurt him if she didn't cooperate. Her knees buckled. Only the big man's arms kept her from crumpling to the floor.

"There you go. Now you figured it out. I knew you weren't stupid, Lily."

His voice lingered over her name, sending chills down her spine.

"You be hearin' something very soon. Then you'll understand how serious my boss really is."

The Cajun backed toward the door. "Take care of her," he ordered the man holding her.

The tall man released his tight hold and grabbed her wrist. She had a fleeting glimpse of his profile before he flipped the afghan from her couch up and over her head.

He spun her around a few times until she stumbled dizzily. Then he lifted her in his arms.

"Don't mess with these people," he whispered. "Do what he said." He knelt and set her gently on the floor, then pushed her. She slid across the hardwood and hit the wall.

Kicking and struggling, she tore at the fuzzy material that blanketed her. Her limbs were weak with fear. She was shaking so badly she couldn't catch hold of the afghan. She sucked in a deep breath, and lint and dust choked her. She coughed, then moaned at the pain in her throat.

Her front door slammed.

Finally she fought her way free of the tangle of knots and yarn. For an instant she crouched there against the wall, hugging the afghan to her chest. Were they really gone?

She held her breath and listened. Silence. She looked around. The apartment was dark. It felt empty.

Barely daring to breathe, she tried to push herself to her feet, but her knees gave way. She collapsed back to the floor, her sore throat contracting around the sobs that erupted from her chest.

She gave up trying to stand and crawled over to her couch, expecting at any moment to be grabbed again. She switched on the lamp with shaky fingers.

Nothing. They were gone.

She huddled in the corner of the couch, hugging her knees to her chest, unable to stop shivering. She was chilled to the bone, although it was September and still summertime-hot in Biloxi, Mississippi.

She didn't know how long she sat there staring at the

front door, terrified they'd return. Sick with the knowledge that they knew where she lived.

Still afraid to trust her trembling legs, she crawled over to the door and reached up to throw the dead bolt. The useless gesture was almost funny. They'd gotten into her apartment once. They could do it again.

She pulled herself to her feet, her body aching with tension, her head woozy with fear. Leaning against her kitchen counter, she chafed her sore arms. Her throat and jaw hurt. She couldn't stop trembling.

What was she going to do? They'd threatened her. Threatened her father.

Dad! The little Cajun hadn't said anything specific, but his implication sent icy fear surging through her veins. His boss had chosen her because she was alone and vulnerable—and so was her father.

She had to check on him. Carefully she walked over to the couch. Where was the phone? It had been knocked onto the floor when she'd bumped her head on the end table. It was halfway across the room.

She moved unsteadily toward it as pain shot through her shoulders. The man who'd held her had been strong. Thank God he wasn't as cruel as the Cajun.

Just as she touched the handset, it rang.

She jerked away with a startled cry and covered her mouth with both hands to keep from screaming.

It rang again. Her temples throbbed. Her heart raced. She forced herself to pick it up.

"Ms. Raines? This is Mary Bankston, night supervisor at Beachside Manor."

Horror clutched at her chest. *No, please!*

"Ms. Bank—" Her voice wouldn't work. She swallowed painfully and tried again. "Ms. Bankston. What's wrong?"

"Don't worry. Your father is fine. But there was a small incident a few minutes ago. Somehow, some papers in the trash can in your father's room caught fire. The nurse on duty put them out immediately, and made sure your father wasn't injured. I can't imagine how he managed to get matches or light a fire. But it's all under control now."

Lily's hand cramped around the phone. "You're sure? You're sure he's okay? I can be there in twenty minutes."

"I don't think he even realizes anything happened. You certainly don't need to drive over here—"

"Yes. Yes, I do." She hung up the phone, old, familiar guilt squeezing her chest.

Her father, a cop, had once been so vital, so big and strong, so courageous. But a gunshot to the head during a liquor store robbery had turned him into a bewildered, docile shell of the man who'd raised her.

He'd survived the shooting, but the loving father who had taught her right from wrong, who'd stressed the importance of truth and justice, was gone.

Unable to speak and barely able to understand rudimentary conversation, Joe Raines seemed to look forward to her visits, but the times were fewer and fewer that his brown eyes lit up with recognition.

The intruder's Cajun twang echoed in her ears. *You be hearin' something very soon.*

Bile burned her throat and nausea made her double over. They'd made their point. They'd already gotten to her father.

Suddenly her head spun and acrid saliva filled her mouth. She stumbled into the bathroom, making it just in time.

Collapsing onto the cold tile floor, she bent her head over the toilet, giving in to the spasms. She gagged and coughed until there was nothing left inside her.

Tears streamed down her cheeks as she flopped back against the wall and wiped her face with unsteady fingers. For a few moments she just cried. She was so scared. So tired.

It was amazing how fragile humans were. And how fast hope could turn to despair. In an instant, everything could change.

About the same time as her father was shot, she'd found out her husband was cheating on her. He'd always been controlling, but she believed in marriage, so she'd tried desperately to make hers work.

He'd asked for a divorce and moved out.

Then, because of the time she had to devote to caring for her father, her fledgling interior design business had suffered.

Still, she'd survived. She'd started over, like so many others.

Then, just last week, she'd begun negotiations to design the interior of a new high-rise being built in Biloxi. She'd started feeling hopeful once again. Strong and safe.

But no more. Today, her life and her father's had changed again. Their lives were threatened.

Her dad's beloved, confused face rose in her mind. He was all she had. And she was all he had. She had to get to the nursing home, to see for herself that he was all right.

She struggled to her feet, her muscles stiff from the

cold tile, her stomach fighting the nausea that still clung to her. She splashed water on her face.

How would she face her father, knowing what she had to do? *Vote not guilty. Let a murderer go free.*

It went against everything he'd stood for all his life. Everything he'd taught her about justice and truth. To protect him, she would have to betray everything he believed in.

She looked at her pale face in the mirror. How could she do anything else?

BRANDON GALLAGHER TOSSED down a straight shot of Irish whiskey and grimaced. The burn felt good, but it didn't wash the taste of self-disgust from his mouth. He slapped the glass down on the counter and nodded at the bartender, then got up and headed for the bathroom.

He splashed cold water on his face, and when he did, his senses were filled with the scent that clung to his fingers. Vanilla and fresh coconut.

He held out his arms and examined the scratches. A ghost of a smile crossed his face.

He turned on the hot water and scrubbed his hands with soap, then rinsed his face. Lifting his head, he met his eyes in the flaking mirror.

"Can't wash away your own stench with whiskey, nor her perfume with soap, can you, Gallagher?" he muttered. He patted his face and hands dry with a paper towel, then he wet a corner of it and wiped the specks of blood off his forearms. She was a fighter. That was good. She'd need to be.

Foshee had carped at him all the way down the stairs and back to Gio's. *This ain't good cop, bad cop, salaud. You too soft. Mais, yeah, I better tell the boss you can't handle it.*

Brand hadn't reacted, although his insides had clenched with worry. He'd prayed he was reading the little Cajun right. Foshee was merely flexing his nonexistent muscles. He wouldn't really go to Castellano.

Feigning unconcern, Brand had just grunted and muttered that there were better things to do with females than rough them up.

To his relief, Foshee had laughed.

You better watch her. Make sure she don' turn tail. You watch her and I watch you. Boss wants to hear how you handle this job.

As soon as he'd gotten free of Foshee, Brand had driven back to Lily Raines's apartment. He was surprised to see her car still there. But just about the time he cut his engine, she'd rushed out and taken off in a spray of gravel. He knew where she was going. To Beachside Manor—her father's nursing home.

She'd definitely gotten the message.

Satisfied that she'd understood the threat Foshee had made, and relieved that she hadn't been hurt by his man-handling, Brand had turned his car around and headed straight here, to the neighborhood bar. He sent his reflection a disgusted glance.

The local watering hole. God love it. His dad would have been proud.

Grimacing at that thought, he pushed his hands through his hair, and went back to his seat at the bar.

He faced down the shot glass filled to the brim with pale brown liquid. The sight of it made his mouth water.

No. He rubbed a hand across his face, feeling the day's growth of stubble and smelling the last faint whiff of Lily Raines's perfume.

He'd come too close too many times to sinking into a bottle, just like his old man. Just like his oldest brother. There were better ways to die.

And there'll allus be worse ones. His dad's slurred Irish brogue echoed in his ears.

"Shut up, Dad," he muttered.

As much as he'd like to use a quart of Irish whiskey to drown the look of terror in Lily Raines's eyes and forget the reason he'd been there to see it, he couldn't afford to.

Three years and thousands of hours of undercover work were on the line. And as of tonight, his career probably was, as well.

Because Giovanni Castellano, the King of the Coast, had ordered "Jake Brand," with Armand Foshee to watch over him, to make sure Juror Number Seven held out for acquittal in Theodore "Sack" Simon's murder trial.

With a sigh, Brand threw some cash down on the bar, turned his back on the brimming shot glass and headed for his car. He maneuvered the dark streets to a private pack-and-mail store that rented post office boxes. The store was closed, but he had a key to the alcove where the boxes were located.

He parked at the entrance and took a moment to roll up the leg of his jeans. Gritting his teeth, he ripped the tape off his ankle and with it the miniature tape recorder that had been a part of him for the last three years.

He massaged his skin where the tape had abraded it, ejected the tiny cassette and inserted a brand-new one. He stuck the tape recorder in his shirt pocket. His ankle could use a rest. He'd tape the device back on his leg first thing in the morning.

He pulled his sock up and his cuff down.

Then he wrote the date on the used tape's label and dropped it into an envelope, unlocked the box and shoved it inside, just as he'd done three or four times a week for the past three years. His fingers encountered a note. A single sheet of paper, folded once. He stuck it in his pocket and grabbed the untraceable prepaid cell phone his contact had left in the mail box.

He dialed the only number programmed into it. The cell phone of FBI Special Agent Thomas Pruitt.

"Pruitt. It's Gallagher." He could hear voices in the background. It sounded like a ball game.

"What's up?"

"I got an assignment today from Castellano."

"No kidding? Hang on."

Brand heard Pruitt tell someone he'd be right back. After a few seconds the background noise lessened.

"Sorry. My kid's baseball game. Go ahead. What happened?"

"Castellano put me with a ratty little lowlife named Foshee. We paid a visit to a juror in the Simon case. Leaned on her hard. Foshee threatened her to vote not guilty, to hang the jury, or something would happen to her father."

"Wait a minute. Castellano gave you this assignment himself?"

"Yep. I got called into his inner sanctum—his table at Gio's. Foshee was there, along with a couple of muscle-heads with machine pistols."

"I'll be damned. Finally! We've waited for three years for a break like this. Who is she? The juror?"

"Name's Lily Raines. She's juror number seven."

"Raines. I wonder if she's related to a guy named Raines I used to know. He got shot on the job a couple of years ago."

"That's him. He's in Beachside Manor Nursing Home. Something happened there tonight. Foshee didn't tell me what, but it was enough to send Lily tearing over there about twenty minutes after we left her apartment."

"I'll check on it."

"How do you want me to handle this? You going to let the D.A. know Castellano's tampering with the jury?"

"How'd you handle it tonight?"

Brand made a rude gesture toward the phone. He didn't like Pruitt. "How the hell do you think? I went along. I didn't know any specifics until we got to her apartment." It had sickened him to have to hold her still while Foshee manhandled her and threatened her. "I tried to keep Foshee from being too rough."

"You did right. You've gotta play along. Three of you undercover for three years and this is the closest we've gotten to Castellano. We had a feeling he would try something during the trial, but this is better than we'd hoped. We can't risk any screwups at this point."

Brand's gut clenched. His lieutenant, Gary Morrison, who had been his contact for his first year undercover, had stressed the importance of not going outside the law any more than necessary. If an undercover cop was going into a situation where he would be forced to commit a felony, his commanding officer had an obligation to extract him.

Brand and the other two officers working inside Castellano's operation were protected up to a point, but they were required to report any illegal activities in which they were involved.

"Yeah, well, you haven't been working with the damn mob for three years. I don't want any screwups, either, but I'd like to know you've got my back once this is all over."

"You do the assignment. I'll protect your back."

Brand blew out a frustrated breath. Pruitt was FBI, and there was no love lost between the Feds and local law enforcement. He wondered if he was being set up to take a fall.

He pulled the microcassette recorder out of his pocket. With his thumb he pressed record and held it near the phone. *Never hurts to have insurance.*

"Gallagher? You there?"

"Yeah. Just thinking. Make sure you understand, Pruitt. I've worked too hard to end up getting my badge yanked for committing a felony."

"Listen to me. The justice department is behind this operation one hundred percent. They've given us carte blanche. Any means necessary. Have you talked to Springer or Carson?"

His fellow officers working undercover. Brand frowned. "Nope. Hardly ever see 'em."

"Well, Carson is working the docks. He's convinced Castellano's moving weapons and explosives in. Springer agrees. Plus, he says they're bringing in illegal aliens."

"Terrorist activities."

"Right. So you're covered on all sides, by justice, homeland security—you know the drill."

Brand did. Job one was to protect his fellow officers. Job two, earn Castellano's trust.

"You think we can get Castellano on terrorist charges?"

"I think so." The excitement in Pruitt's voice was obvious through the phone line. "If we can, he'll go away for a long time and the careers of everybody involved will be assured."

Yeah, Brand thought. You mean *your* career. But he didn't say anything.

"So do what Castellano wants you to do. You'll be protected. We'll have plainclothes watching you and the lowlife, what's his name?"

"Foshee. Armand Foshee."

"Right. Foshee. The task force will step in before the verdict. We'll probably pull Foshee in on some lesser charge. You, too, so your cover isn't blown. The trial will end in a mistrial, but it won't come down on you. Trust me, we've got plenty on Simon. We can pick him up on another murder charge before he sets foot outside the courtroom."

Pruitt made it sound easy. But then he wasn't out in the field. He didn't have to worry about who got hurt.

Brand's thoughts returned to Lily Raines. Terrified, trembling, her soft breasts pressed against his forearms, her dark, shiny hair tickling his nose. "What about the woman? What about her father?"

"They're not your concern. We'll take care of them."

"The hell they're not. I'm the one leaning on her. I don't

like it. I don't like the threats against her father, either. Can't the police give him protection?"

"We don't want to blow your cover or endanger your juror. We can't afford to let Castellano see any change in her father's care. You just do your job."

Damn. He didn't like working with the FBI. They played everything too close to the vest. He rubbed his neck. "Should I call you back to confirm?"

"No. You've got the go-ahead. I'll take care of making it right with the justice department." Pruitt disconnected.

Brand turned off his cell phone and stuck it in his pocket. Then he stopped the tape recorder, ejected the cassette and held it between his thumb and forefinger.

Like he'd told Pruitt, he'd worked like a dog to pull himself out of the chaos of his childhood. He was not going to let anything ruin his career as a police detective. It was all he had.

He tossed the cassette a couple of inches into the air and caught it in his fist. Insurance. He had Pruitt on tape promising to cover his butt.

As he walked back to his car, he stuck the cassette in his pocket. His fingers encountered the note he'd picked up from the mailbox.

After climbing into the driver's seat, he scanned the note and cursed. He shook his head as he crumpled the note in his fist. His request for two days' leave to go to Alexandria, Louisiana, for his father's funeral had been denied.

He'd expected it. He was in too deep with the Gulf Coast mob to risk disappearing even for a day or two. Especially now that he had finally penetrated the impenetrable armor surrounding Giovanni Castellano.

His eyelids stung and he blinked rapidly. Pop had been dying for a long time. The alcohol had finally killed him. But his death dredged up memories of another death, that of his oldest brother, Patrick. There was nobody to blame for Pop's death except Pop himself.

But Patrick was another story. Brand's brother had gotten in too deep with gambling and drugs. He owed Castellano more money than he could ever pay, so the mob boss had ordered his execution to make an example. For all Brand knew, Sack Simon had pulled the trigger.

Patrick was the reason Brand had become a cop. The reason he'd volunteered for this particular assignment in the first place.

He sighed. Now to catch Castellano, he had to let the assassin who may have killed his brother go free. God, he hoped Pruitt was telling the truth when he'd said Simon wouldn't walk out of the courthouse before they arrested him again.

He cranked his car and pulled away. He had to be up early tomorrow to go to the courthouse with Foshee.

The justice department had damn sure better protect his badge, because he had no choice but to do this. For more than one reason.

Sure, he was doing it to avenge his brother's death and to protect his fellow undercover officers. But there was a third reason. As he drove back to his apartment, the remembered scent of vanilla and coconut filled his nostrils.

Lily Raines needed him. She had no one else to protect her.

Chapter Two

The empty halls of the courthouse mocked Lily as the click of her heels echoed through the silent corridors. Within an hour, these same halls would be buzzing with activity, and yet she'd still be alone.

She hadn't slept a wink all night. She'd been afraid to turn off the lights, and every noise she heard sent fear slicing through her.

Her father's bland, trusting face haunted her. He was so helpless, and Castellano was ruthless. He'd gotten to her dad inside the nursing home. How could she keep him safe anywhere?

Still, she'd done her best. She'd stalked into the nursing home, indignant and worried, and demanding that whoever had let her father get hold of matches should be let go. She pulled it off with just enough of a touch of frantic daughter that she'd managed to back the head nurse into a corner.

She had agreed to move Lily's dad next to the nurse's station so they could keep an eye on him.

She also promised Lily that she would find out who had

left matches lying around and have them fired. Lily didn't bother to tell her that she wouldn't find anything.

Lily stepped through a set of double doors, and passed one of the assistant district attorneys assigned to the Sack Simon case. The medium-height young man looked smart and capable as he nodded absently at her. Lily wondered what he would do if she told him Castellano had sent thugs to threaten her.

She went through the door into the jury room. It was empty. She managed to make a pot of coffee, but spilled a little when she poured herself a cup. Standing at the door, she searched the face of each person who walked by. She recognized some, such as the ADAs, one of the court reporters and a couple of police officers who knew her father.

Every single time someone walked past, her heart sped up and she prayed for the courage to reach out—to ask for help. But each time she gripped her cup more tightly and remained quiet. None of them could protect her against the most powerful man on the Gulf Coast.

How could this happen in this day and age? Years ago, organized crime had been rampant up the eastern seaboard, along the Gulf, even in the Midwest. Back then the mob was into drugs and prostitution, loan-sharking and money-laundering.

Giovanni Castellano was of a totally different breed. He owned legitimate businesses, paid health insurance for his employees. He was even on the committee for the renovation of the Gulf Coast.

According to defense counsel, Castellano and everyone who worked for him, including Sack Simon, were model citizens.

Whatever illegal activities Castellano was involved in, they were hidden behind a facade of honest business practices. And that meant it would be almost impossible to find anyone who could protect her against him. Who could she trust?

Icy fear crawled up her spine. Even if she could get protection for herself, what about her father? Giovanni Castellano, the King of the Coast, was untouchable.

It was the Gulf Coast's worst kept secret that Castellano's money came from illegal activities such as smuggling and loan-sharking. Yet somehow he'd never been indicted by the police. Her father had always complained that Castellano had a politician in his pocket.

"Lily Raines? Little Lily? Is that you?"

She jumped and almost spilled her coffee again.

A man in an ill-fitting brown suit smiled at her. "Didn't mean to scare you," he said.

Swallowing the urge to back away, she smiled quizzically. "Yes. I'm Lily Raines. Do I know you?"

"Bill Henderson. I used to be on the job. Worked with your dad." The man's florid face lit with a smile as he tugged on his belt, adjusting it over his pot belly.

"Of course, Officer Henderson. It's been a long time."

Henderson's smile faded. "Sure has. Last time I saw you, you were still in high school. Call me Bill. I heard about your dad. Been meaning to get by to see him, but you know how it is. I'm real sorry. He was one of a kind."

She nodded. She remembered her dad talking about Henderson. *Good people,* her father had called him.

"You're on jury duty?" Henderson asked, raising one gray eyebrow.

"The Sack Simon case."

"Whoa! That rat bastard." Henderson shook his head. "He's guilty as sin. Everybody knows he's Castellano's top hit man. Got at least fifteen notches in his gun."

Lily nodded and glanced up and down the hall. As a juror on the case, she wasn't supposed to talk about it with anyone. "You said you *were* on the job?"

"Yep, I took my twenty-five and retired. I do some private work here and there, when I'm not fishing."

"What brings you to the courthouse?" she asked, her thoughts racing. He knew her dad. He'd been a police officer for twenty-five years. She could trust him.

"Divorce case." He made a face. "I've gotta testify. I took the pictures the wife is using to squeeze a bundle out of her soon-to-be ex-husband."

Lily's pulse thrummed in her ears. Maybe he could help her. If she knew her father was safe, she could vote guilty. Then, as soon as the trial was over, she and her dad could move far away from Castellano's reach.

She glanced around again. "Can I ask you a question, Bill?"

"Sure. Anything for Raines's girl." Henderson laughed. "You need a ticket fixed, I'm your man."

A nervous smile lifted the corners of her mouth. "Not exactly." She took a deep breath just as the double door opened.

It was the bailiff. Lily blew her breath out in frustration. He would reprimand her if he caught her talking in front of the jury room.

Two of her fellow jurors entered behind the bailiff.

As she watched the bailiff approach, Lily decided to go ahead. If she was going to reveal what had happened, what difference did it make if the bailiff overheard?

"Bill, what if I told you that—" The door opened again, and when she saw who entered, terror sheared her breath.

Sauntering in behind the jurors was a skinny man with sun-darkened skin and coal-black eyes. He leered at her and bared his teeth.

Just like last night. It was *him.* The Cajun. Lily's throat closed up. She couldn't breathe at all.

Behind him came another man—taller, broad-shouldered and confident. It was the Cajun's tall, menacing partner. His gaze met hers and he frowned. His eyes were a piercing blue, she noticed abstractedly.

He gave a quick, almost imperceptible shake of his head.

She froze, unable to look away from his intense blue gaze. Her fingers tightened reflexively around the ceramic mug in her hands. He was warning her.

She looked from him to the Cajun.

"Lily?" Henderson raised his bushy brows.

She sucked in a long breath and forced herself to face her dad's former colleague. "N-nice to see you," Lily stammered as the bailiff stopped in front of her.

"Good morning, Ms. Raines," the bailiff said.

Lily nodded jerkily.

"I'll let my father know you asked about him," she said

to Henderson, stepping backward into the room. Her voice was too loud, but she couldn't help it.

Please don't say anything, she silently begged Henderson.

More people entered the hallway. The Cajun and his partner passed the door. The Cajun's black eyes sparkled and he made an offhand gesture at the level of his neck. Lily read his message loud and clear. She touched her throat where the point of the Cajun's knife had pricked her the night before.

The other man kept his gaze averted, but she felt his presence, his overwhelming attention, and she remembered that he'd stopped the Cajun from hurting her—twice.

She watched the back of his head as he followed the Cajun through the door into the main corridor of the courthouse. Just as he stepped inside, his head angled, as if acknowledging her gaze.

She shuddered, her stomach flipping over. They had to be here checking on her. There was no way she could escape them. They would be there through every minute of the trial. They'd watch her when she went in and out of the jury box. And anytime they wanted to, they could hurt her father.

She ducked inside the jury room, her stomach rebelling at the black coffee she'd swallowed. How would she make it through the day, much less the whole trial?

"WHAT THE HELL'S the matter with her?" Foshee said.

Brand bit back a curse. He knew exactly what Foshee was talking about.

Lily looked as if she might faint and fall right out of her chair. Her face was pale and her eyes had dark circles under them. Her dark hair hung limp and straight around her face, and she clutched the armrest of the jury box chair so hard he could see her whitened knuckles.

He bent his head and whispered to the shorter man. "She didn't sleep. She's probably so scared she's sick, and I can see the bruise you left on her jaw from here." *You stinking little bully,* he added silently.

"Whassup wi' you, Brand? You sweet on her?" Foshee grinned, showing crooked, stained teeth.

"Nah. Guess I just know better than you how to handle a lady."

"Zat so?" Foshee angled his head. "Mebbe I let you *handle* her after I finish wit' her, eh? 'Cause if she don' straighten up, she get herself kicked off the jury. See how the DA's watching her?"

Brand clenched his fists. He'd already noticed. The Assistant District Attorney in charge of the case had been watching Lily all morning, probably worried about the same thing Brand feared. She was so pale and drawn. Was she about to faint?

It was time for the ADA's summation to the jury. He looked at Lily again, then whispered to his co-counsel. Brand could imagine what they were saying.

They wouldn't want a sick juror, or one who was terrified, helping to decide the fate of Sack Simon. They had to be sure all the jurors were capable of coherent thought and rational reasoning.

Brand had been there through the jury selection and *voir dire.* There were two very competent alternates waiting in the wings. The ADA could easily replace Lily.

After another few seconds of whispering, the ADA nodded at his colleague and stood. "Your honor, may we approach?"

Brand stiffened. This was about Lily. He knew it.

He wished he could catch her eye, but after last night, anything he did would be interpreted by her as a threat. If he even made eye contact with her, she *would* faint.

The judge and the two attorneys consulted while eleven jurors fidgeted. Lily sat stiff and still, her too-wide eyes watching the lawyers and the judge talk. Every so often, her gaze would flicker toward either him or Foshee.

He saw her throat move as she swallowed nervously.

Get yourself together, Lily, he begged her silently. *They'll kill you.*

Then the defense attorney glanced their way with a tiny smile.

The lawyers returned to their seats and the judge rapped his gavel. "We'll recess until tomorrow morning at ten o'clock."

Brand let out a deep sigh.

"What's going on?" Foshee asked in surprise as they stood while the judge left the bench.

"We just dodged a bullet. I'm guessing the ADA was asking to excuse juror number seven."

Foshee's black eyes glittered. "We gonna have to pay our girlfriend another visit?"

"No," Brand said quickly. "Look at her. She looks better already. She's exhausted and scared to death. A good night's sleep and she'll be okay."

"*Mais, oui.* We call her, eh? Tell her good-night?"

Brand shook his head. "Leave her alone, Foshee. You

hurt her. You scared her half to death. Trust me, she got the message. She'll come around."

They filed out of the courtroom with the rest of the curious onlookers and walked around to the side of the courthouse to stand at the door where the jurors exited. They mingled with the media and the onlookers.

Brand stood beside Foshee, dreading the moment when Lily walked out and saw them waiting for her.

She was the last one through the door. Her face was still pale, and she clutched a tissue as she was escorted to the door by a security guard.

"Sure you're okay, honey?" the uniformed woman asked her.

Lily nodded and smiled faintly. "Thank you. I feel much better. I appreciate the ice water. It's probably just a bug. I'll be fine by tomorrow I'm sure—" Her gaze met Brand's and she faltered.

Brand lifted his chin and sent her a faint nod.

Her gaze flickered from him to Foshee. She brought the hand holding the tissue to her mouth and hurried past them, catching up with a middle-aged man—juror number three, if Brand wasn't mistaken.

"Okay. We gotta check in," Foshee said. "See if the boss wants us to follow her."

"She's not going anywhere. Other than maybe to see her father."

Foshee squinted up at him. "You sure do know a lot for a two-bit bouncer."

Brand glared down at the little man. "Castellano obviously thinks I do. He gave me this job."

"*Mais, non.* He give *me* the job. He give you to me to train. And I guarantee you he ain't gonna like how you're so 'fatiated with our girl."

Brand shrugged. "It's your fault she's too scared to function. Give her a break. She's got a lot of thinking to do."

The Cajun laughed, showing his crooked teeth. "That she does, *brau.* That she does."

BRAND DIDN'T EVEN GLANCE at the neighborhood bar on his way to his cover apartment that night. Hanging out with thugs and lowlifes put a bad taste in his mouth, and he knew from his childhood that it couldn't be washed away with whiskey.

As soon as this assignment was over, he was done with the undercover racket. He'd take homicide. Working with plain old murderers. At least that way he could feel like a cop, instead of some lowlife.

In his one-bedroom apartment, he turned the radio to an oldies station and grabbed a bottle of water from the small refrigerator.

Flopping down on the sagging couch, he glanced at his watch, took a long drink of the cold water, then sucked in a dose of courage. He needed to call his brother, Ryan.

Ryan was four years older than Brand, and he'd often protected Brand against their father's alcoholic rages.

He picked up his cell phone and dialed. It took several rings for Ryan to answer.

"Hey, Ry."

"Hey." Ryan's voice was remote.

"How'd it go?" Brand sat forward and propped his elbows on his knees.

"How do you think it went? It was a funeral. *Dad* missed you."

The jab hit home. Brand's chest constricted. "Yeah, well, lift a glass to him from me," he shot back.

Ryan was silent.

"Come on, Ry. You know why I can't be there. I asked. They turned me down."

"Did you?"

"What do you mean, did I? Hell, yeah, I did."

"Hard to believe they wouldn't let a guy go to his own father's funeral."

"Cut it out, Ryan." Brand stood and paced, clenching and unclenching his fist. Maybe it was a bad idea to call him so soon. The funeral had been today.

"You know better than that. I'm undercover, and I just got my first break in the case. I can't afford to blow the operation by disappearing. There are lives at stake."

"Yeah. You're so damn important. Everybody was asking about you. Mom's made you into a hero around here—big bad cop who's too busy to see his own father buried."

"Well, at least I saw Patrick," he threw back.

Damn it. It happened every time they talked. The same old argument. The same old hurts.

Ryan felt guilty because he had been away at school when their oldest brother, Patrick, was murdered. Thirteen-year-old Brand had found him lying across the doorstep of their house, dead from a single bullet to the head, with a dollar bill stuffed in his mouth.

Castellano's calling card.

"Yeah, and you finally got what you wanted. Revenge." Ryan's voice was rough with emotion.

"Come on, Ry. I'm not doing this for revenge. I'm doing it because it's the right thing."

"Sure you are. That's why you chose to isolate yourself from your family, and why you went so deep undercover that you're becoming one of them." Ryan took a breath. "I saw Aimee the other day. She's engaged."

"Aimee?" Brand's gut tightened. He'd been thinking about giving her a ring when the undercover assignment had come up. He'd only seen her once in the past three years, and he'd had to pretend he didn't know her.

"Sorry."

"Yeah. Me, too. Is Mom okay?"

"She's making it." Ryan's voice sounded less tense. He'd needed to blow off some steam, just like Brand had.

"I think we might stay for a while. Mom's having a fit over the baby. Cassie can help Mom clean out Dad's stuff, and I might see what kind of contracting jobs are available."

"Stay? In Alexandria?" A pang in Brand's chest made him realize how much he'd miss his brother. Even if they didn't always get along, even if he hadn't been able to see much of him while he'd been undercover, he'd always known Ryan was just across town if he needed him.

"What about the house? Cassie's studio?"

"I've got a guy watching the house. And Cassie hasn't used the studio since she got pregnant. Fumes from the oil paint and turpentine. I'm thinking about selling it."

"Right. Tell her I'm sorry I haven't gotten to see the baby. I didn't want to put y'all in danger."

"Sure. We understand."

Brand cleared his throat. "Gotta go, Ry. Tell Mom I'll call her when I get a chance. Tell her I love her."

"Try to stay out of trouble—okay?"

"Always do." Brand disconnected, blinking hard. He didn't know why his dad's dying had affected him. The old man had either been in a rage or passed out drunk during most of Brand's life. Brand had learned early that the best thing to do was stay out of his way.

He finished his water and shot the empty plastic bottle into the trash can like a basketball.

Thoughts of his father led to thoughts of Lily Raines, and the horror in her eyes when she'd realized Foshee was threatening her father. Her obvious love and fear for her dad haunted him. The way she'd frantically rushed to his side as soon as he and Foshee left made Brand feel guilty and somehow deprived.

He'd felt a secret relief when his request to go to his father's funeral had been denied. And that had made him feel even more guilty. But the truth was, he hadn't seen his dad in five years, and as far as he was concerned, that wasn't nearly long enough.

For him, family equaled pain. His childhood memories were those of crying, yelling, fists and rage. He'd spent his boyhood hiding behind Ryan or hanging out with kids from school—kids whose fathers didn't trash the house if dinner wasn't on the table when he got home. Mothers who didn't jump at every little noise, or stare out the window with haunted eyes in the late afternoon. Kids whose parents were normal.

Then there was his oldest brother. Poor Patrick had followed in his father's footsteps, all right. He hadn't even made it to thirty.

He didn't remember ever feeling the way Lily obviously felt about her father. He had no concept of that kind of love. A place inside him ached—hollow, empty. He ran his hand over his face trying to wipe away his maudlin thoughts.

But he couldn't wipe away the vision of Lily with her big, frightened brown eyes and her soft, vulnerable lips. He couldn't get the smell of vanilla and coconut out of his nostrils.

Damn it, he wished he could warn her how necessary it was for her to be strong and brave. This was life and death. He hoped she knew that.

He longed to tell her he would do anything in his power to keep her safe, but that she *had* to make it through the trial without faltering.

He ached to touch her again, this time to comfort her, rather than scaring her half to death. But if he broke cover, not only would her life and her father's be forfeit, he and two other cops could die.

LILY PULLED INTO her parking lot and glanced at the dashboard clock. She'd intended to be home before dark, but her father had seemed so happy to have her visit she hadn't had the heart to leave early. He'd nodded sagely when she mentioned Bill Henderson. He'd even repeated his name.

She'd told him about Castellano's hit man, and the men who'd threatened her, but he'd just nodded again.

For a moment she sat in her car as her eyes filled with tears of grief. Her dad had once been so strapping and smart.

Ever since her mother had died when she was twelve, she and her dad had depended on each other. She didn't count the months right after her mother's death, when her dad had retreated into his own grief. For the most part, he'd been a great dad. He'd taught her how to defend herself, how to handle a gun, so she'd never be helpless. He'd listened when she'd cried with her first broken heart. And he'd been there to cheer when she'd graduated college with a degree in interior design.

"I need you now, Dad," she whispered. "More than ever. I need to know what to do."

The father who'd raised her would be appalled if he knew she was even considering voting not guilty. Not with the kind of evidence the prosecution had against Simon. He'd have waved away the danger.

I can take care of myself, he'd have told her. *And I can take care of you.*

But there was no way he could do that now. She had to take care of him. And if that meant letting a killer go free—so be it.

She slapped the steering wheel with her palms, and wiped her eyes. Enough of acting like a baby. She'd find a way to get help. There had to be someone she could trust.

A car's headlights glared in the rearview mirror, causing her heart to leap into her throat. She'd broken one of the basic rules of personal safety. Don't park the car and sit in it. She needed to get inside and put the chain on the door.

Imaginary spiders crawled up the back of her neck as she grabbed her jacket and purse. She shuddered and glanced around. Then she took a deep breath, jumped out of her car and ran up the steps to her second-floor apartment.

As she unlocked her door, her shoulders tightened in awful expectation of the feel of a heavy hand.

She looked over her shoulder. Nothing. She pushed open the door and sighed in relief when she saw her living room bathed in the light from the lamp she'd left on.

The attack came from her left.

A hand clapped over her mouth.

No! Not again! She kicked and bit and tried to scream for help.

The hand pressed tighter and a rock-hard arm pinned hers to her sides. She flung her head backward, trying to head-butt her attacker, but he dodged and pressed the left side of his head against the right side of hers, then pushed her inside and kicked the door shut.

She smelled soap and mint. Alarm sent her heart racing out of control.

"Shh! Lily!" His voice was raspy and soft. "Be still. Shh. Stop struggling."

Desperately, she stomped his instep.

"Ow. Stop it! Listen to me." He lifted her as if she weighed nothing and carried her into the living room.

She was so helpless, so weak. None of the defensive moves her father had taught her worked against this man. She struggled, but he was like a massive tree—immovable, sturdy, unbending.

His hand over her mouth loosened and she took a breath to scream.

"Don't." The hand tightened again, as did the arm across her chest. She could barely breathe.

She went limp, tears of frustration and fear filling her eyes.

"Promise?" his whisper rasped in her ear. His stubble scraped her cheek.

She tried to nod.

"This is serious, Lily. Don't try anything. Don't yell, don't hit, and for heaven's sake, don't bite."

She nodded again. Her chest burned for air. She sucked as much as she could through her nose. It wasn't enough.

His hand on her mouth eased up.

She gasped.

He slid his hand down past her jaw, which was still sore from the Cajun's punishing fingers the night before, to her neck. He didn't grab her, he didn't punish. His thumb touched the minuscule wound left by the Cajun's knife.

In another world, in another time, she might have thought his fingers were gentle, caressing. But here and now, she knew who he was. He'd been here last night. He'd held her—let the Cajun touch her. A quiver of revulsion rippled through her.

He'd threatened her with a searing glare and watched her like a hawk in court.

Lily felt sick. A cold sweat broke out across her face and neck.

He tightened his hold. "Don't faint on me, Lily. I need you to be strong. You have to listen to me." His breath was hot on her ear.

She tried to turn, but he held her in place, tight up against his unyielding body. The heat he gave off burned her to her core.

"You almost got kicked off the jury today. Do you know that?"

She swallowed against his fingers, which still held her throat in an ominous caress. Any second he could tighten them and choke her.

"Do you?" he snapped.

She nodded jerkily.

"You've got to be brave. You've got to stop looking like a doe facing a rifle."

His low voice sounded earnest, as if he was worried about her. She closed her eyes and fought the urge to give up, to lean against him and stop struggling.

But she knew he couldn't be trusted. He was the enemy. He had hurt her. He'd held her while the Cajun had hurt her.

"That's pretty much what I am," she said shakily.

"You've got to look confident. Can you do that? It's the only way you'll survive."

"Wha-what are you talking about?" she croaked, confused by the urgency in his tone.

His hands slid down over her sleeveless top and tightened on her bare upper arms. He turned her around to face him.

His face was grave, his blue eyes burning with intensity as they searched her face. He lifted one hand and traced the bruise the Cajun had left on her jaw with a surprisingly gentle brush of his fingers.

Conflicting emotions swirled inside her. He'd grabbed her, threatened her. Why was he being so kind? Was it a trick? Was the Cajun waiting outside?

She stiffened, and cut her eyes over to her front door.

"Shh. It's okay. He's not here."

Her gaze shot to his, suspicious. "He sent you?"

"No. I came on my own, to warn you." His left hand touched her chin. "Listen to me, Lily. Jury summations are tomorrow. They won't take long. The prosecution thinks they've got the case sewn up. Get up in the morning, shower and fix your hair. Put on makeup. Do whatever it is you do to look good."

Tears burned her eyes. She shook her head. "I can't do it. I can't sit there in front of the judge and the lawyers, with the families of people Sack Simon killed watching me with their hopeful eyes. I can't betray them."

"You've got to. You have to walk into the jury box like you own it. Don't give the ADA a reason to kick you off the jury. If you do, your father will die." His face darkened. "You'll die."

She blinked and the tears streamed down her cheeks, down her neck. His thumb moved, rubbing the dampness into her skin, touching her in a way he had no right to. Making her feel safe when she knew she wasn't.

"Don't cry, Lily. Be strong."

She sobbed.

"Shh." He bent his head and put his mouth against her ear. She sniffled and was hit with the scent of him—soap and mint.

He'd brushed his teeth to come threaten her again. A little hiccuping giggle burst up from her chest.

"If you can be strong, if you can hold out, I promise you I'll keep you safe."

"You?" she spat, jerking her head away from his seductive whisper. "I'd rather die."

He sighed and his eyes went storm-cloud gray. "Then you will."

He turned her around and pulled her back up close against him again. His soft, ominous whisper burned through her. "Think about it, Lily. It's your only chance. It's the only way your dad will survive."

He pushed her toward the couch.

She stumbled and fell onto the cushions. By the time she'd righted herself, he was gone.

The smell of soap and mint lingered in the air.

Chapter Three

When the jurors filed into the jury box, Brand's mouth fell open. He'd told Lily to do whatever she did to look good, but he hadn't expected much.

Whatever she'd done, it had worked. She looked like a different person. Gone was the pale skin, the fearful, darting eyes, the entwined fingers.

Her brown eyes sparkled, her hair was shiny and wavy and her skin glowed under the harsh fluorescent lights of the courtroom.

Her transformation was amazing. *Too amazing.*

A sick dread spread through his gut. She didn't look like this because he'd warned her. He eyed the pugnacious lift of her chin, the determined line of her jaw, and his mouth went dry.

She looked like a new woman because she was. She'd come to a decision.

Beside him, Foshee whistled under his breath. "I reckon you was right about one thing, *brau*. She jus' needed some rest. Looks like a whole new woman."

Too much like a whole new woman. *Ah, Lily, what have you done?*

As the DA got up to make his closing arguments, Brand shifted and cursed under his breath for Foshee's benefit. "Damn it, I gotta take a piss," he muttered.

The little Cajun looked at him sidelong. "Mebbe I better go wit' you."

"Oh, yeah? I don't think so. I'll be right back."

Brand stood and slipped out of the courtroom, aware of Lily's eyes following him. He didn't dare look at her—he wasn't sure why.

Standing alone on the courthouse steps, out of earshot of anyone who might walk up, he pulled out his cell phone and dialed the preset number.

"Pruitt."

"It's Gallagher."

"Isn't court in session?"

"Yeah. This is important." Brand kept an eye on the courthouse doors. He didn't want to be surprised while talking to his FBI contact. "What's happened?"

There was a pause on the other end of the line. "I don't know what you mean," the FBI agent said finally.

"I think you do. Yesterday Lily Raines was about to fall out of her chair, she was so scared. Today she looks like a new woman."

"Maybe she got some rest."

"Did she talk to someone? Has anyone talked to her?" Anger blossomed in his chest. "Damn it, Pruitt. If something's up, I need to know."

"I swear, Gallagher, I don't know a thing. She didn't talk to the DA's office, or I'd have heard. Maybe you're over-reacting. Take a chill-pill."

Brand commented on what Pruitt could do with his chill-pill. "What about Springer and Carson? Anything going on with them?" He rarely ran into the other two officers who were working undercover with Castellano's operation.

"They're checking in daily. Nothing from their end. Look, I told you I'd protect you, and I will."

"Can you protect her, too?"

"We're on it. We figure it'll take about three days for the jury to figure out she's not going to change her vote to guilty. We'll be there to intercept you and Foshee, and to rearrest Simon. It's all going smooth as silk."

"I hope to hell you're right."

Brand disconnected and headed back inside. He sat down next to Foshee, who sent him a suspicious look.

"What took you so long?" he whispered.

"Got a call." In case Foshee had looked out the court-house door and seen him on the phone, he needed to stick as close to the truth as possible.

"Yeah?"

"Ex-girlfriend. Wants to hook up."

Foshee grinned. "You could hook me up."

"That would serve her right," he muttered.

Foshee scowled at him.

Brand listened to the DA's monotonous drone. *Crap.* In typical lawyer fashion, he was telling the jury what he was about to tell them. Then he'd tell them, then he'd tell them what he'd just told them.

After him, the defense attorney, paid for with Castellano's money, got to put on his own performance.

And Brand was stuck here sitting next to Foshee, with his garlic breath and his bad teeth.

It was going to be a long day.

THREE DAYS LATER, retired police officer Bill Henderson drove his wife's van toward Beachside Manor Nursing Home. He'd been surprised to hear from Joe Raines's girl the other night. Lily had sounded frantic, scared to death.

He shook his head, amazed at what Lily had told him and ashamed at how hard he'd tried to weasel out of helping her. Especially now.

Like he'd told Lily, he'd done his twenty-five years on the force. He was looking forward to a lot of years of sitting out on the water in his little boat, fishing and drinking beer and just being happy to be alive.

He'd decided not to take any more private jobs. Most of them were just this side of sleazy. He didn't like spying on cheating spouses or rounding up deadbeat dads.

His pension was enough, with his wife's income from teaching, to keep them comfortable.

He turned onto the street that wound back around the bayous to the grounds of Beachside Manor. Funny name for a nursing home that was nowhere near the beach.

Lily had asked him to go to the nursing home on Friday morning and pick up her father for what she'd termed a "day trip." She said she'd called the nursing home and given her permission. All he had to do was show photo ID.

"Take him somewhere, Bill. Please. I'll pay you. Take

him up to Jackson to a hotel. Just for a few days, until this trial is over. Then I'll come get him and we'll be out of your hair. Please. Do it for a fellow officer. You know he'd do it for you."

As soon as she'd said those words, Bill had known he was sunk. So here he was, about to abduct a buddy of his who didn't even know his own name. Like he'd promised Lily, he'd lied to his wife—told her he had to be out of town for a few days on a case.

He'd asked Lily what was going on, but she wouldn't tell him. He had a feeling he knew. Another reason he'd tried his best to refuse. This had something to do with Sack Simon's murder trial. Therefore it had something to do with Giovanni Castellano. He sure as hell didn't want to tangle with Castellano.

The idea made Bill very nervous. He ran a finger under his tight collar and checked his weapon, which he'd stuck in a paddle holster at his back. He rarely carried it anymore, even though he had a permit.

The road to Beachside Manor was asphalt, with a narrow shoulder that quickly dropped off into a swamp. He kept his van toward the middle of the road as he rounded a steep curve.

A car was stopped in the middle of the road, and a woman in a tight skirt and a tighter blouse with the top buttons undone waved both arms at him. She looked hot and harried.

Bill slowed down and pulled up beside her. He lowered his passenger window. "Got car trouble, miss?" he asked.

"I don't know what's wrong. It just stopped, right here

in the middle of the road. I'm supposed to be at the nursing home to pick up my mother." She gestured behind her with a hand holding a cigarette.

"Hop in and I'll give you a ride." Bill pressed the button that unlocked the doors. As soon as he did, the driver's door jerked open and a hefty guy stuck a gun into the folds of skin at his neck.

"Wha—?"

"Don't move, Henderson."

Bill didn't move. Sweat popped out on his forehead and under his arms. He should have been prepared for this. Twenty-five years on the force had taught him better than to be caught by the oldest trick in the book.

"What do you want? Money?" Stupid question. It wasn't money. The gunman had called him by name. This was Castellano's doing.

Icy sweat gathered and trickled down his back and under his arms. His mouth went dry as a bone.

"Come on, man, I'm not hurting anyone. I'm just visiting a buddy."

"Too bad you won't get to see him. Did you think we wouldn't have a bug on his daughter's phone? She wouldn't know, but you, Henderson. You're an ex-cop. You should know better."

Bill shook his head as sweat dripped down his face. "Don't, please. I got a wife—"

It was the last thing he ever said.

SEVERAL HOURS LATER, in the confines of the jury room, eleven pairs of eyes stared at Lily in disgust and anger. It was the end of the second day of jury deliberations and they were all hot and tired and sick of each other.

To their surprise, the judge had sequestered them. The trial was too public, he'd said. The media was all over it. He wasn't going to risk a mistrial.

He'd instructed them that they could either have a family member bring them clothing or go to their home accompanied by a court official to pick up their things.

Lily had been given five minutes to gather her makeup, clothes and toiletries. No mail. No newspaper. No laptop.

The foreman stood at the head of the table, waiting. "Well, Ms. Raines? Did you hear me? We still have eleven guilty votes. I trust that now, after you've had several hours to review the evidence, you are prepared to admit that Sack Simon is indeed guilty?" The insurance salesman managed to sound irritable and defeated at the same time.

Lily glanced at her watch. Bill Henderson should have picked up her father hours ago. It was scary as hell not being able to talk with him to be sure everything went as planned.

The slight bulk of her cell phone pressed against her thigh. She'd hidden it in a secret pocket of her handbag, and had stuck it in the pocket of her black suit skirt this morning with the ringer turned off.

She knew she'd be in legal hot water if the bailiff discovered that she had it, but she couldn't afford to be without some means to contact Bill Henderson. She'd given him her number. Of course, she'd had no time alone to call out or check for incoming calls. Even during the two hours she'd requested to go over the evidence again, stalling for time, a security guard had sat with her.

It wasn't that she didn't trust Bill. He was as reliable as they came. He would never let down a fellow officer. Plus, he and her father had been good friends.

By this time he and her father should have arrived in Jackson safe and sound.

As soon as she got out of here, she'd call and be sure everything had gone smoothly. Then she'd run home, pick up her important papers and the small stash of cash she kept hidden in her closet and head north to Jackson.

She'd pick up her dad and keep going north until she got to Memphis or even farther—so far away that Castellano's influence wouldn't reach them. She'd change her name if she had to. She'd started over before. She could do it again.

She looked at each of the jurors in turn, hoping the desperation and uncertainty she felt wasn't reflected on her face.

It all comes down to what's right, Lilybell. You can't outrun your conscience.

I know, Dad. I'm doing it. You'd be proud of me.

"Ms. Raines, please don't make us stay here another night. It would be a travesty of justice if we had to go out there and report that we're deadlocked. Surely even you can't still believe the evidence is inadequate."

Lily took a deep breath, praying that Bill hadn't had any trouble, wishing there was a way she could know for sure. But he had promised her he wouldn't let her down. He was a former police officer. He could take care of himself and her father.

She clasped her hands together in her lap and took a deep breath. "I've studied the DNA evidence and the fingerprint, and the testimony," she said, her voice trembling with anxiety. "I vote guilty."

BRAND AND FOSHEE were waiting on the courthouse steps when someone shouted that the jury was back. Foshee dropped his cigarette and stomped on it.

"Let's go. This oughtta be good."

Brand's phone rang. He stiffened.

Foshee turned. "Who's that? Your ex-girlfriend again?"

Brand forced a smile. "Yeah. Go on. I'll catch up."

Foshee's black eyes narrowed. "Nah. I'll wait."

Brand looked at the caller ID and felt his heart rate pick up. It was Pruitt.

"You know I'm busy, *sweetheart*," he growled, turning the volume on the phone down. Foshee was standing uncomfortably close.

Pruitt laughed shortly. "Okay, I get it. You can't talk. Got a report that an ex-cop buddy of Raines's was shot in his van on Lindon Road earlier. The road to Beachside Manor."

"Damn it!" So that's what Lily had done. She'd tried to get her father away from the nursing home, away from the long reach of Giovanni Castellano.

She was going to vote guilty!

Sweat prickled his scalp and stung the back of his neck. He racked his brain for a way to give Pruitt a clue. "You know what that means, don't you? Is everything else all right?"

"Yeah. A car came along and interrupted the killers. The

driver called 911. The killers took a couple of potshots at the Good Samaritan, but he wasn't injured. He got a partial tag number, too."

"Well, that's good, I guess. So what are you going to do now?"

Foshee's curious black eyes snapped as he did his best to eavesdrop. Brand turned away.

"We'll pick up Raines. Put him in protective custody."

"You'd better hurry."

"I'll take care of it. You lay low."

"I can't—"

Pruitt disconnected.

Brand punched the disconnect button on his phone and burst out with a string of insulting adjectives describing his fictitious ex-girlfriend.

"Come on. We gonna miss the verdict."

Brand pocketed his phone with unsteady hands, his mind racing.

If—no, when—the verdict was read, Lily's life wouldn't be worth a plugged nickel. He had to do something. He couldn't guarantee that he'd gotten that across to Pruitt. Surely if the FBI man had sense enough to put her father under protection, he had a plan for rescuing her.

"Whassa matter wit' your girlfriend?"

Brand looked at the little Cajun, trying to process what he'd just said. "Girlfriend? Oh. My ex. She let my washing machine overflow."

"So you did hook up." Foshee laughed as they filed into the courtroom.

Brand's neck muscles knotted and his chest grew tight

as the jury filed in. Then they all stood while the judge entered and got settled behind the bench.

He asked the defendant to stand.

Theodore "Sack" Simon, nicknamed because of his habit of hiding his gun in a paper bag and shooting through the bag, stood, smoothing his tie and adjusting the sleeves of his custom-made suit. He glanced back over the onlookers, caught Foshee's eye and smiled.

Brand grimaced.

"Jurors, have you reached a verdict?" the judge asked the foreman.

"We have, Your Honor."

The bailiff took the verdict from the hands of the foreman and walked it over to the judge.

Brand couldn't tear his gaze away from Lily. She was pale, and her fingers were white-knuckled. Her eyes were clear though, and as he studied her, she met his gaze. A ghost of a smile touched her full lips.

No, Lily! But it was too late.

His pulse hammered in his ears. His fingers tingled. He didn't think he'd ever been as utterly terrified as he was right now, not even when he was seven and his father had broken his mother's nose, sending blood spatter flying, spraying all over him.

The judge read the note and handed it back to the bailiff, who gave it back to the foreman.

Brand's pulse hammered louder and louder. He doubled his left hand into a fist and pushed the knuckles against his lips.

Foshee chewed a dirty fingernail.

Simon nervously picked an invisible speck off his sleeve.

"What say ye?" the judge recited.

"On the single count of murder in the first degree, the jury finds the defendant, Theodore Simon, guilty."

Simon swayed. His lawyer steadied him and whispered in his ear.

The courtroom erupted in noise. The judge's gavel echoed again and again, the sound reverberating inside Brand's skull.

Guilty. Guilty. Guilty.

Foshee let out a little squeak.

Lily's throat moved as she swallowed, but there was a look of pride on her face, a blush of triumph in her cheeks that sent dismay coursing through Brand's veins like blood. He clenched his fists, straining to appear unconcerned, while his stomach clenched and sweat prickled the back of his neck.

She didn't know she was dead.

FORTY MINUTES LATER, by the time Lily walked out the side door, most of the media had already grabbed the other jurors for sound bites. She lowered her gaze and headed straight for her car. As she stepped off the curb into the parking lot, a woman brushed against her and shoved a note into her hands.

She stopped and turned, but the woman quickly disappeared into the crowd.

Lily looked down at the note. The words leaped off the page.

Henderson is dead. Your father is—

"Oh, God, no." She stumbled, reaching out to steady

herself against the hood of a car. Her head spun. Her stomach turned over.

Bill Henderson was dead. Was somebody playing a sick joke? She looked at the block printing again then turned the note over. Her father was what?

There was nothing on the back of the note.

"Dad—" she whispered.

Was he dead, too? She covered her mouth, afraid she was going to faint or throw up. Had Bill Henderson been murdered? If so, it was her fault. Her stomach churned and she swallowed hard. She couldn't be sick. She had to get to the nursing home.

Papers. Money. She needed to go by her apartment to get the forms necessary to have her father discharged. *No time to waste.* If she delayed it would be too late. She tried to straighten but her head spun.

She heard footsteps behind her. She whirled and found herself staring into a camera lens as a zealous reporter shoved a microphone in her face.

"You were one of the jurors. How do you feel about the verdict?"

Panic clogged her throat. She pushed the mic away and shook her head.

"Ma'am. Why did it take two days to reach a verdict? Were you certain from the beginning that you were going to vote to convict?"

"Please leave me alone," she begged as she searched for her keys in her purse. Finally her fingers closed on them, but her hands were shaking so violently she almost dropped them.

"The viewers would like to hear your statement, Ms.—" The reporter consulted a sheet of paper. "Ms. Raines. You were juror number seven. Tell us what your thoughts were—"

"No!" She pressed the remote and unlocked the driver's side door. "I have to go. Get out of my way."

She climbed in and started the engine as the reporter shot her a venomous glance, then composed his face and turned to the camera.

Lily put the car in gear and pulled away. Her hands were white-knuckled on the steering wheel as she scanned the scattering crowd.

Where were the Cajun and Blue Eyes?

Dear God! They were probably already on their way to the nursing home.

She dug in her pocket for the cell phone she'd smuggled into the jury room. She dialed Beachside Manor. The phone was busy.

Cursing, she tried again and again. How could the line be busy this long?

As soon as she got to her apartment building, she vaulted out of the car and ran for the steps. She rammed the cell phone back into her pocket. She had to get her papers and the small stash of money. Then she'd call the nursing home again.

She'd ordered them not to allow any visitors except for poor Bill Henderson. But Castellano had gotten to him once before, with the fire in the wastebasket. She had no doubt the crime boss could get to him again.

As she put one foot on the stairs, she had the ominous sense that there was someone behind her.

Her breath caught. She started to turn. All at once her legs were knocked out from under her. She hit the ground hard, bumping her head, and dropped her keys.

Desperate to find them, she groped blindly along the ground.

"Get up."

She couldn't see. Couldn't stand. Pain and fear doubled her over.

She'd failed. Despair blanketed her.

Dad! She'd tried to protect him, tried to do the right thing. Would God let her death be easier because she'd tried so hard? Would He care for her father because none of this was his fault?

A heavy shoe nudged her in the ribs. "Pick her up, *bioque.*"

The accent sunk in. It was the Cajun with his knife and his stinking, stale breath. Raw fear burned through her. He would enjoy killing her.

Hands lifted her. Blue Eyes's hands. At least he wasn't mean. Maybe he'd keep the Cajun from torturing her.

She let herself be picked up. She didn't have the strength to fight, not even when the Cajun grabbed her bruised jaw in his punishing little fingers.

"You ain't so smart after all, girl. You know what? Your dad, he's already dead."

She didn't react outwardly, although her heart squeezed painfully. Blue Eyes's arms tightened around her in a protective gesture.

"Here, *bioque.*"

One of Blue Eyes's arms loosened as the Cajun handed him something.

"You do it. This'll be your initiation. You'll be blooded. Slit her throat. If you can." The Cajun laughed.

Then he grabbed her hair and twisted her head back and to one side. Lily couldn't hold back a whimper.

He ran a finger across her exposed neck. "Right there."

She felt the cold, sharp edge of a knife against the skin of her neck. Too close. Too sharp. Her skin tightened, as if shrinking away from the deadly blade.

She couldn't even swallow. If she moved, the razor-sharp edge would sink into her skin.

Blue Eyes rested the hand holding the knife against her collarbone. She felt his hand tremble, and a dreadful hope bloomed inside her.

She closed her eyes. He didn't want to kill her. Or maybe he was just nervous about his first murder. The Cajun had said it was his initiation.

"Well?" the Cajun prodded. "You gon' stand there all night?" He jerked on her hair and she felt the blade slice into her skin.

Her breath scraped her throat. *God, please let me die bravely, and please take care of my father.*

BRAND'S VISION TURNED red with rage. Foshee's cruel punishment of Lily had caused Brand's hand to slip. He'd accidentally cut her.

One quick glance and he knew the cut was relatively minor, thank God. But he'd had enough.

He knocked Foshee's hand away from Lily's hair with his forearm. At the same time he threw her sideways, out of the way. Then he coldcocked the Cajun with a sharp left.

Foshee dropped to his knees.

Brand held the knife in his fist and pummeled Foshee's face, once, twice, until the slimy rat collapsed, unconscious, in a heap on the ground.

Then he turned to Lily.

She'd risen to her knees, and was struggling to stand.

Brand tossed the knife aside and grabbed her. Whispering an apology that he knew she wouldn't believe, he pulled a Flexicuff out of his back pocket and strapped her wrists together in front of her.

She didn't say anything. She just watched him the way his mother had watched his father. Like a whipped pup watches its master.

The fleeting thought cut Brand to the bone. He met her gaze.

"It's okay," he whispered, but as he'd predicted, she didn't believe him.

Her brown eyes held a heartbreaking resignation. They swam with tears.

The idea that she thought he was going to kill her filled him with self-disgust, but he didn't have time to explain.

He'd already heard a couple of shouts. Above his head an apartment door slammed. There were witnesses. The police were probably already on their way.

He grabbed Lily by her hands and pulled her up, then wrapped an arm around her. He half carried her to his car. As he opened the passenger door, her weight collapsed on his arms. She'd fainted.

He tossed her into the passenger seat, locked the door, rounded the car and climbed in the driver's side. With his heart pumping and his senses on hyper alert, he stomped the gas and took off.

Once he'd cleared the parking lot and hit the main road, he took a second to glance over at her. Blood had run down her neck to stain her white blouse.

Rage and regret choked him. He'd done that. He'd cut her. But at least he'd saved her from death. For now.

He gave a brief thought to Foshee. Would the Cajun get away before the police got there? Brand hoped not. He hoped the perverted lowlife got himself arrested.

It might buy him some time to get Lily to a safe place.

Thinking about Foshee reminded him of Pruitt's promise. What had happened to the officers who were going to pick up him and Foshee after the verdict? For that matter, why hadn't Simon been rearrested?

His anger at Foshee expanded to encompass Special Agent Pruitt. The jerk had lied to him.

LILY'S NECK STUNG. She tried to touch the cut but something was wrong with her hands.

She opened her eyes. She was in a car, a fast car. And her hands were bound.

What had happened?

Then she remembered.

The note. The knife.

"Dad!" She pushed herself up and blinked at the driver. "Oh, my God!" It was Blue Eyes. She whirled, looking for the Cajun.

"Settle down, Lily. Your dad's okay." The man with the blue eyes sent her a worried look. "How's your neck?"

"Where's the Cajun?"

"Back there on the ground."

She remembered Blue Eyes pummeling him. "Dead?"

Blue Eyes shook his head. "No."

She swallowed against nausea. Her throat ached and her mouth grew dry with panic. "Where are you going? What are you going to do with me?"

He glanced over at her. "I'm not sure." He sounded angry.

"Who are you? Did you kill Bill Henderson?" Her voice broke. "Did you kill my father?"

A grimace crossed his face and the muscles of his jaw tightened. "No."

She looked at him narrowly. "You had that woman hand me that note, didn't you? You killed Henderson."

He shook his head. "Not me."

Fear like ice water surged through her veins. She shivered. "I don't believe you."

"You don't have a choice. You have to trust me."

"Trust—" she choked on the word. "You cut my throat."

He didn't react, unless his chin lifted a fraction. It could have been a trick of the light, though.

"Are you going to kill me?"

His eyes cut over to her, then back to the road. "Probably not."

His calm answers and bland expression frightened her. Maybe more than the Cajun had with his cackling laugh and his disgusting, punishing hands.

A shudder racked her body. "Where are you taking me?"

He didn't answer. His profile was stoic, unmoving as he maneuvered his car quickly through side streets that she didn't recognize.

"Tell me *something*. You're scaring me."

He nodded. "I know." His voice seemed to hold a tinge of regret.

Her lip trembled. Her heart hammered in her chest. "I don't understand. Where's my father? Please talk to me!" She didn't believe his assurance that her father was all right. He'd held her, helped the Cajun threaten her. She couldn't trust him.

How could she go on if her father had died because of what she'd done?

"Okay, Lily. I'll tell you something." His quick, intense look turned her limbs to jelly. In some ways he was more frightening than the Cajun.

"Because of you, one man is already dead. Now, by voting guilty, you may have five other deaths on your conscience, including your own."

Chapter Four

Brand cursed silently. He'd told Lily the truth when he'd said he had no idea what he was doing. He'd acted on the protective instinct he'd felt for her from the first time he'd been forced to restrain her. He hadn't been able to stand by and let her be harmed.

His hand went to his pocket where he felt the weight of his prepaid cell phone. He wanted to call Pruitt and demand to know why he'd reneged on his promise. Nobody had showed up to intercept him and Foshee before the verdict.

Pruitt had lied to him. He should have known better than to trust the FBI. Bureaucratic asses. Pruitt was probably waiting on some damn paperwork, or approval from his bosses or something.

Meanwhile, Foshee had pushed him too far. He'd known Foshee was ready to kill Lily if she voted to convict. Hell, he'd probably been instructed to kill her either way. She knew too much to be allowed to remain alive.

He'd had to save her. Now his cover was blown and his fellow undercover officers were in danger. When Castellano found out that Brand was a cop working undercover, he'd turn his scrutiny on his other employees. Springer and Carson wouldn't stand a chance.

Brand slammed the heel of his hand against the steering wheel and cursed out loud.

Beside him Lily started, then shrank against the passenger door. Her fear of him infuriated him.

"What the hell were you thinking, voting guilty? You signed your own death certificate, and your father's." He glared at her. Her eyes had little flecks of gold in them, he noticed as they filled with tears.

She blinked and tears spilled over and ran down her cheeks. "So my father's dead?"

Her small, heartbroken voice cut him to the quick. He shook his head, considering what he should say. He wasn't about to tell her he was a cop. Not until he figured out what he was going to do with her.

"I don't think so."

Her face drained of color. "You don't?" She tried to lift one hand, but the Flexicuffs hindered her. More tears dripped down her cheeks.

Brand glanced in the rearview mirror as he turned onto the street that ran behind his apartment house. There was a narrow driveway that led almost up to his back door. He'd never told anyone who worked for Castellano where he lived, but they knew his car, and he was sure they could find his apartment if they wanted to.

He didn't dare linger. He'd be there just long enough to get his gun and badge. Then he had to figure out what to do with Lily.

"Where are we going?" Lily asked, sitting up. "Please. Take me to see my father."

"Please—could you shut up for a minute?" he growled as he backed into the driveway and stopped the car at his back steps. "I need to think."

His apartment was in an old clapboard house that had been divided up by its enterprising owner. The house had escaped the ravages of weather and time, but suffered from the owner's long-term neglect.

Restrained by the Flexicuffs, Lily fumbled with her door handle. Brand quickly rounded the front of the car and opened it for her. He hooked a hand around her arm and lifted her out. She started to struggle, but he squeezed her arm and pulled her close as he shut the door.

"Don't." He scowled at her and felt a grim satisfaction when her throat moved nervously. She stopped trying to get away from him, but her body grew so rigid it felt like she might break. The spark of terror in her eyes told him she still thought he might kill her.

She sucked in a deep breath. He put his fingers gently against her lips to stop her from screaming.

"I said don't. That means don't struggle. Don't scream. Don't do anything except what I tell you to do." He snaked his arm around her and guided her up the concrete steps into the house. The hallway was dark. She stumbled as they crossed the threshold and a drop of liquid splashed onto his hand.

She was crying. He could imagine the direction her thoughts were taking. For all she knew he was one of Castellano's enforcers.

As his fingers twirled his keys, feeling for the one that unlocked his door, he squeezed her shoulders with his other hand. "Don't worry. I'm not going to hurt you."

"You already did," she spat.

He pushed her through the door ahead of him.

Lily lost her footing but caught herself on the kitchen counter, wincing as the plastic thing binding her wrists cut into her skin. Fear bubbled up from her chest, stealing her breath.

Turning, she flung her hair out of her eyes and studied the man who'd abducted her. He tossed his keys on the counter without looking and kicked the door shut behind him with a familiarity that struck her like a blow.

This was his apartment.

Alarm streaked through her. "Who are you? Why did you bring me here?"

He frowned down at her and shook his head slowly. "That's a good question."

She studied him warily. "Then answer it. What do you want from me?"

He walked over to the front window and looked out, then checked his watch. "Believe it or not, I don't want anything from you."

She stared at him, her head swimming with his contradictions. He'd saved her life, but he'd also held her still while the Cajun had groped her. Suddenly her memory flashed on the glint of the knife he'd held against her throat, and the sharp sting as the blade drew blood.

Her hand reached up to touch the wound, but the strip of plastic stopped her.

"Ouch," she uttered softly as she pressed her wrists together to keep the plastic from cutting her skin.

"Here," he said, crossing the tiny living room in two strides. "Let me get those off you." He pulled out a pocket knife and opened it, then hesitated, his blue eyes searching her face. "If you'll promise me you won't run."

"Where am I going to go? I don't even know what street we're on."

"Good. Although I'd have thought your father would have taught you the importance of observing your surroundings."

Her mouth went dry at his mention of her dad. She was so afraid for him. "He did," she snapped. "I was too scared. I let my guard down."

He took her hands and slid the knife blade up under the plastic tether. It popped apart, exposing a pair of matching red marks on her wrists.

A curse hissed through his teeth as he lightly traced the inflamed skin of her wrist with his forefinger. He bent his head. "I don't think the skin is broken, but you're probably going to have bruises. You struggled too much."

She jerked her hand away and resisted the urge to rub her wrists. "When can I see my father? Take me to him. Or at least let me call him."

"No time. We can't stay here." He grabbed her arm. "Come on. I need to take a look at your neck. See how bad it is. Then I've got to—" He stopped, eyeing her sidelong. "There's something I've got to do."

"I need to know whether my father is—whether he's okay."

He flipped an ancient chrome dinette chair around from the table. "Sit."

She lifted her chin and stood firm, fighting to keep her lip from trembling.

"Look, Lily, we don't have much time. Do what I say and I promise I'll check on your father."

"Why?"

His lips flattened into a thin, straight line. "Why what?"

"Why would you do that? Why did you turn on your partner? Why'd you bring me here? What's your name? Tell me *something*."

He sighed. "Brand."

"Brand? That's your name?"

A curt nod was her only answer. "Now sit!" He glowered at her from under lowered brows.

She sat.

Brand watched her as he reached up into the kitchen cabinet for his first-aid kit. He didn't have much, just the essentials: alcohol wipes, antibiotic ointment, bandages and Steri-Strips to use in the place of stitches if necessary.

He pulled out another chair and sat down in front of her. He ripped open an alcohol wipe, then wrapped his right hand around the side of her neck and urged her chin up with his thumb.

She cringed when he touched her, which sent a wave of self-loathing coursing all the way down to his toes. He clenched his jaw and reminded himself that it was better if she was afraid of him. Better for her, and easier for him.

The cut on her neck was ugly. It was about an inch and

a half long. Luckily for her, it wasn't deep. He touched it with the alcohol wipe.

She flinched.

"Sorry. Hold your breath."

He cleaned the cut as air hissed through her teeth. His gaze followed the tense line of her jaw up to her full lips and petal-soft cheeks. His thumb slid lightly across the curve of her jaw as he berated himself for being an idiot.

As if to punctuate his self-contempt, his body hardened in reaction to the feel of her supple skin and the sight of her small pink tongue as she nervously moistened her lips.

He imagined that tongue touching his, those full, smooth lips pliant and yielding as she responded to his kiss.

Damn it! He jerked his hand away, causing her to flinch. She was terrified of him. Even if he wanted to, he'd never kiss her. A twinge of regret pricked him.

He shook off the dangerous, distracting thoughts.

He needed to get in touch with Pruitt. He had to let him know what he'd done, and make sure Pruitt took steps to protect Springer and Carson. He also wanted to check on Lily's father, and arrange to get the two of them into a safe house.

Because the minute Foshee woke up, Castellano would know about her jury vote, and her life wouldn't be worth a plugged nickel. She'd defied Giovanni Castellano. Brand knew the King of the Coast wouldn't stop until he'd made her pay.

"Turn your head," he said gruffly. "I need to close the edges of that cut and put a bandage on it."

Lily obeyed. She was confused by the way her captor

was acting. He acted like he was angry with her, but just now when he'd touched her neck and jaw, his touch had felt like a caress.

And she still didn't know what he intended to do with her. Had he saved her from the Cajun's clutches so he could have her for himself?

Fear slithered up her spine and she recoiled, straining away from his hands. When she did, he sat back.

She touched the bandage. It seemed huge. "How bad is it?" she asked.

"Just a scratch." He closed the lid of the first-aid kit. "Wait here. I'll be right back." He picked up his keys and locked the double dead bolt on the back door. With an arch look he pocketed the keys.

"I need to go to the bathroom," she said.

He shook his head. "We've been here too long already. You'll have to wait."

"You'll be sorry."

He cursed. "Go on, then. Hurry. I'll be right outside."

She looked around the efficiency apartment. There were only four doors. The front and back doors, one that was closed and beside it, the bathroom door, which stood ajar.

She went inside and closed the door behind her. As soon as the latch snicked into place, she stepped to the far corner of the room and pulled her phone from her pocket.

Her trembling hands almost dropped it. Gripping it tightly, she hit the preprogrammed button for the nursing home, almost crying with the combination of relief and fear. *Please let him be all right.*

A voice answered. "Beachside Manor, Blue Wing. May I help you?"

"Yes," she whispered. "This is Lily Raines. I need to check on my father, Joe Raines. He's in room 118."

"I'm sorry, ma'am, I can't hear you."

Lily glanced at the door, then bent over the phone and repeated her request.

"Just a moment please."

"No, don't—" The woman had put her on hold.

Lily pressed her clenched fist against her mouth. *Hurry, please,* she whispered silently. With another glance at the door, she turned on the water in the sink.

She was running out of time. She had to make a choice. As a lump grew in her throat and her eyes stung with tears, she set her jaw and pressed the disconnect button. She had to cover her mouth to keep from crying aloud. She'd cut off contact with her father.

Dear God, please keep my dad safe.

A sharp rapping on the door made her jump. *Brand.*

"Come on, Lily." His voice carried easily over the running water. "You're taking too long. Don't make me come in there."

Standing with her back to the far wall of the bathroom, Lily debated whether she'd made the right choice. Her thumb hovered over the nine.

BRAND HAD RETRIEVED his badge and gun and changed into jeans and running shoes as soon as Lily shut the bathroom door. He'd stuck the weapon in his belt and his badge in his wallet. Then he'd pulled on a long-sleeved shirt, leaving the tail out to hide the bulk of his weapon.

Now he paced back and forth in front of the closed bathroom door, staring in frustration at his cell phone. He knew he ought to call Pruitt, but he couldn't shake the feeling that there was something wrong with the whole operation. The assignment Castellano had given him was too perfect.

He'd worked as a bouncer in Gio's for over a year, and in all that time the crime boss had barely spared him a glance. He'd ingratiated himself with the other bouncers and Castellano's private bodyguards, hoping for a chance to work his way into the boss's good graces.

Then finally, Castellano had sent for him. But the importance of the assignment Castellano had given him seemed too good to be true. Foshee's curious attitude had increased his suspicions.

Finally, Pruitt had lied to him. He'd hung him out to dry.

None of it made sense, and all of it smelled like a setup.

His fingers keyed in a familiar number. His lieutenant's cell phone. He knew he could trust Gary Morrison. They'd worked together for five years, including the first year he was undercover with Castellano. But then the task force had replaced all the local law enforcement with federal officers. Brand was reassigned to Pruitt.

He winced as an annoying tone screeched in his ear.

"We're sorry, but the number you have dialed is not in service at this time."

What the hell? A frisson of alarm skittered through him. He double-checked the number. It was correct.

His pacing took him back to the bathroom door. He stopped and raised a fist, prepared to knock again. Lily was taking far too long.

He heard something. He frowned, listening. She was talking.

"Damn it," he muttered as he shoved the door open.

"—don't know the address—" he heard her say as the door slammed into the wall.

She had a cell phone.

In one swift motion he cornered her and ripped the phone out of her hands. He closed it, disconnecting the call.

"That was not smart. Who'd you call?"

Her face was pale as she shook her head. "Nobody."

"Come on, Lily. Give me some credit. I heard you say you didn't know the address. You called 911, didn't you?"

Her tongue darted out to moisten her lips. She shook her head.

"You're a really bad liar. Let's go. If the cops got a bead on your phone, they'll be here any minute." He took her by the arm and guided her out of the bathroom and back into the kitchen, where he ran water into a bowl and dropped her cell phone into it.

"No! Wait!" she cried, trying to push him aside and reach for the phone.

He caught her hand and stopped her.

"You've ruined it! Oh, God. It had the phone number of the nursing home. I need to check on my father."

"I told you, Lily. He'll be all right."

"Why should I believe you?"

He shrugged. "I can't think of a reason, except maybe that you don't have a choice."

"Will you tell me now what you're going to do? Are you going to kill me, rape me? Hold me for ransom?" She gave a brittle laugh. "Don't waste your time. There's nobody to pay the—"

Brand held up a hand. "Shh."

"What—"

He put his palm against her lips. "Quiet!"

A car had stopped out front. He stood still and listened. Footsteps on concrete, then the sound of the door to the hallway opening. God bless that creaky door.

"They're here. Let's go." He took hold of her arm and pushed her ahead of him toward the back door. He peered out through the window curtains. *Nobody.*

Outside, he closed and locked the back door just as a crash echoed through the apartment. They'd broken in through the front.

Lily heard it, too, because she started and looked over her shoulder.

"That's Castellano's men. We gotta get out of here."

Her face drained of color. "Castellano—?" she mouthed.

Nodding, he deposited her in the passenger seat, confident she'd stay put, then skirted the front of the car.

As he opened the car door, a figure rounded the side of the house.

"Here! Out back!" the guy yelled and lifted an automatic pistol.

Brand ducked behind the car door and drew his weapon. "Get down!" he barked at Lily as a spray of bullets exploded from the man's gun.

Brand rose and fired off two quick shots. He saw another man circling the house. At the same time, wood splintered as a third man broke through the back door.

He fired again, several times, and ducked as the thugs unloaded more rounds on them.

Keeping his head down, he climbed into the driver's seat, quickly inserted the key and started the car. Lily shrieked as slugs shattered the rear window. He burned rubber.

"Are you all right?" he shouted to her.

She was crouched down in the passenger seat. Out of the corner of his eye he saw her nod.

Relief spread through him. Over the roar of his engine he heard shouts and a car engine revving. Glancing in the rearview mirror, he looked down the barrels of two weapons trained on them.

Lily raised her head and turned in her seat to look out the back window.

"Get down!" He reached for her arm. "Down!"

A rain of bullets zinged past them. A metallic thud echoed through the car. Lily cried out and put her hands over her head.

He hoped like hell that wasn't the gas tank. Jerking the steering wheel to the right, he turned onto the street off the alley.

She moved to sit up.

He pressed his palm against the back of her head. "Stay down. They saw which way we went. They'll be right behind us. They may even have the place staked out."

Sure enough, just as he braked at the first stop sign, a car pulled out. He floored the accelerator and ran the stop sign right in front of an oncoming car.

Lily had burrowed into the far corner of the seat. She cowered, her arms wrapped around herself, her hands clenched into fists.

He spared her a glare, but he didn't have a hand to wrestle her back down in the seat. He needed both hands on the wheel and all his attention on the road while he whipped around corners and cut through alleys.

Good thing he knew all the back alleys of Biloxi from his teenage days.

A glance in the rearview mirror told him he'd lost their pursuers for the moment, but he had to make sure they didn't pick up the trail again.

He turned the car toward the Back Bay. They could hide in an abandoned warehouse where kids used to go parking years ago. He'd been there a few times.

It had been old and creaky way back then. He hoped it hadn't been demolished.

Keeping an eye out for Castellano's thugs, he drove a winding route to the gravel road fronting the warehouse.

Lily watched Brand maneuver the car with expert ease. His hands were steady and competent on the steering wheel. His jaw was set and his blue eyes darted between the road and the rearview mirror.

The past days had played hell with her nerves. Now she was hostage to one of Castellano's musclemen and dodging bullets. She had every right to be terrified.

She was scared all right, but somehow not of the man next to her. For reasons she couldn't begin to fathom, he was risking his life to keep her safe.

When he finally slowed to a normal speed, she sat up warily. "You're sure those were Castellano's men?"

"Pretty damn sure."

"What if they were the police?"

"They weren't."

"How do you know?"

He sent her a hard glare as he turned left onto a gravel road. "The police wouldn't open fire without warning," he said shortly.

His biting responses frustrated her. She looked around. The big-city atmosphere of Biloxi had disappeared. The road they were on was deserted. Only a few buildings lined the road and they looked abandoned.

He slowed down just before the road ended at the edge of a bayou. When he turned onto a dirt driveway and drove into a dark, dilapidated warehouse, fear froze her heart.

As the car entered the darkened interior of the building, its headlights snapped on.

"What are you going to do now? Who's here?" she asked as he turned the car around so it faced the open warehouse door.

He stopped the car and cut the engine, still silent.

Lily clenched her fists and sighed in irritation. "I don't understand any of this. I thought you worked for Castellano. What made you beat up your partner and abduct me?"

His face was shadowed but his gaze pierced her. "I'd think you'd have figured that one out by now. I beat up Foshee because he was ready to kill you."

She shivered. "I know that. What I can't figure out is why you turned on him."

He scowled at her. "I thought it'd be damned inconvenient if you bled all over my new jeans."

"Okay, fine, Brand. Or is it Mr. Brand?"

"Just Brand."

"Great. Brand. You abducted me to save me from that little dirtbag. So if you're so hot to save me, why aren't we at the police station right now? Wouldn't that make more sense than holing up in some abandoned warehouse?"

He drummed his fingers on the steering wheel, then nodded without looking at her. "Yeah. It would make more sense—if I trusted the police."

She stared at him. He'd run from Castellano's men. And he wouldn't go to the police. His actions and his annoying habit of not answering her questions didn't inspire trust, either. Something was wrong with this picture.

"Are you a fugitive or something?"

He turned his head and sent her a dark look. "You could say that."

His words were ominous. He was a mass of contradiction. He had frightened her out of her wits more than once. He'd threatened her life, and done everything Foshee had told him to do, up until the point where the Cajun had demanded that he kill her.

He'd rescued her from certain death and apparently appointed himself her protector. Or had he? She still couldn't bring herself to completely trust him, no matter how safe his presence made her feel.

The awful question still hovered in her brain. Had he taken her for himself? Was he a killer or a sexual predator? A deep sense of helplessness engulfed her.

Brand could do anything to her. He was a man, and he outweighed her by at least eighty pounds. He could break her in half or assault her with no effort, and there was nothing she could do about it.

She'd heard stories of how people had saved their own lives by talking about themselves, forcing their captor to look at them as a real person and not just an object to be played with.

Lily swallowed hard. She didn't know how to begin. "What did you do?"

Not a great start, Lilybell, her father's voice said in her mind.

Brand forced his breath out in a whoosh. "What did I do? Hell. I've done a lot of things in my life."

"But you ended up working for Castellano."

He nodded. "That's right."

"And you don't trust the police."

"Nope."

"My father was on the job. He'd almost completed his twenty-five when he was shot."

He squeezed his eyes shut for an instant.

"But you already knew that, didn't you? You also knew he was in a nursing home, helpless to defend himself. His condition is one of the reasons Castellano chose me as the juror most likely to cave."

He fidgeted and shrugged his shoulders. "Look, Lily—"

"He responded to a liquor store robbery in progress. Alone. He called for backup, but when he got there, he heard shots so he went in. The kid was sixteen. He shot my father in the head. The doctors thought he was going to die."

Her small, hurt voice embedded itself in his heart like a splinter. He grimaced inwardly. He didn't want to hear her heartbreaking story of her beloved father. He didn't want to listen to her at all.

He had to figure out what he was going to do. He thought about calling the police station for his lieutenant, but too many people knew him. They'd know his voice.

By now the news media probably had the full story of Lily's abduction, complete with their descriptions. He hadn't seen anyone around the apartment complex when he and Foshee had grabbed her, but he'd heard that slamming door, and he'd heard shouts. Somebody probably saw them tear off in his car.

He was surprised Pruitt hadn't tried to contact him. Maybe the FBI agent was worried that he'd been picked up by Castellano's men, and he didn't want to blow his cover.

Maybe.

"He's been in the nursing home for two years, and he's only getting worse."

Lily was still talking about her father. Her voice was small and brittle. Her chin was in the air, emphasizing the curve of her lovely, graceful neck. Her eyes stared upward and she blinked rapidly, obviously trying not to cry.

Brand's insides squeezed in sympathy. "I'm sorry about your father. All I can tell you is he's probably fine."

She rounded on him, her dark eyes snapping. "You cannot possibly know that. Unless—" She gasped. "Unless you were the one who was supposed to kill him."

"Lily, think about it. What use is your father now? You've already voted guilty. Your father's death wouldn't do them any good. If anything, they'd want to leave him alive hoping you'd go see him. Castellano doesn't like to have his orders disobeyed. He'll have men watching the nursing home. Somewhere out there is a bullet with your name on it."

Her brown eyes widened as she absorbed the real horror of what he was saying. Her hand flew to her mouth and a tiny sob escaped her lips. "Bill Henderson is dead and it's my fault," she whispered breathlessly. "I asked him to pick up my father and take him to Jackson and wait for me there."

"So that's how Henderson got involved. What the hell were you thinking?"

"I thought if I got my dad away from Castellano's reach, if I knew he was safe, I could vote guilty. Oh, God, I got Bill Henderson killed, and I still don't know if my father is safe."

"You thought Jackson was far enough to get away from Castellano? That's only two hundred miles."

She nodded miserably. "I didn't know what else to do."

Brand's throat tightened. What would it be like to care that much for someone? To have had a father who cared, who'd been there all the times a kid needed his dad?

"I believe your father is safe," he said quietly, watching enthralled as her face lit up, her cheeks blushed with rosy color and the tense line of her lips relaxed.

Damn, she had great lips.

"I hope you know what you're talking about. Will you take me to see him?"

He grimaced. "If I can," he said. It wasn't actually a lie. If a miracle occurred and he could safely take her to the nursing home, he would. But miracles were few and far between, especially for a cop on the run.

"So, Brand, is there a bullet with your name on it, too?"

He met her gaze. "I wouldn't doubt it."

"Does that mean we're both fugitives? We're in this together?"

Together. Not likely. In order to save her life, he'd been forced to break the code of the lawman—protect your own. A cop didn't put a fellow cop in danger—ever. But he had left her father vulnerable, unprotected. Lily already feared and mistrusted him. If—no, when—she learned he was a cop, she'd hate him for putting her father's life in danger.

Chapter Five

Lily fidgeted. It was getting late. The sun was about to go down. She could tell from the long shadows around the warehouse. On the far side of the open expanse, Brand leaned against the wall, watching the road from underneath the partially open door. They'd been here at least an hour.

Her imagination had run the gamut of reasons he'd brought her here to this deserted warehouse. Was he waiting for someone? Waiting for dark to kill her and dispose of her body? Hiding from Castellano?

She'd cycled through panic, defeat, anger. Now she was exhausted. She wished that whatever was supposed to happen would happen. It would be better than this ceaseless waiting.

He stuck his hands in the back pockets of his jeans and cocked one hip. Lily let her gaze roam over his body.

She hadn't had much chance to look him over, although she had noticed he was a good-looking man. He was in jeans and a white long-sleeved shirt with the tail hanging out. He'd changed out of his suit while she was in the bathroom, she realized suddenly.

She knew why he wore the shirt. He was hiding his weapon. Lily had been around guns all her life. Her father had taught her how to shoot. He'd taught her to respect deadly weapons. She'd only gotten a glimpse of Brand's weapon, not enough to know what kind it was.

She took in his broad shoulders and sturdy legs, and the casual ease with which he leaned against the wall. He looked perfectly relaxed, but somehow she was certain that every muscle in his body was poised for action.

With the shirt and the snug jeans that hugged his thighs, he didn't look nearly as big as he'd felt when he'd restrained her while Foshee had threatened her. But she'd been afraid for her life, and both of them had seemed like monsters.

Brand didn't look like a monster now. He looked capable, confident. He was tall and lean with well-developed muscles.

She'd already been on the receiving end of his piercing blue eyes. His features were sharp and honed, and faint stubble emphasized the strong line of his jaw.

He didn't look like a mob enforcer. But looks could be deceiving. Lily knew that all too well. Her ex-husband hadn't looked like a controlling, cheating jerk, but that's what he was.

Brand straightened and Lily's pulse quickened. Was someone coming? She clenched her fists in fearful anticipation, but all he did was pull out his cell phone and dial a number. After a few seconds he jabbed a button and shoved the phone back into his pocket with a scowl.

Who was he trying to call? She swallowed against the lump of fear that grew in her throat. Surely it wasn't Castellano, she thought hopefully, or he wouldn't have run from the mob boss's gunmen who broke into his apartment.

He propped himself back against the wall, his attention on the road outside.

She squirmed. She was nervous as a cat. Taking a deep breath, she tried to calm her racing heart and relax her tense muscles. She needed to stop imagining all the bad things that could happen to her and think rationally. She was a cop's daughter, after all.

What would her father do? In his prime he probably could have taken down both abductors and handcuffed them on the spot. A sad smile curved her mouth as she pictured that, quickly followed by a sick fear that twisted her gut and burned her throat. Her father was so vulnerable now. She had no idea if he was safe, despite Brand's assurances.

Come on, Lilybell. Think like a cop.

She looked around the interior of Brand's car. It was a Dodge, one of the sporty models. There was nothing stuck above either visor, nothing in the map compartments and no papers or trash littering the floor. In fact, there was nothing personal at all about the spotless interior.

Glancing up at Brand, whose eyes were still on the road, she opened the glove box. The only thing inside was the owner's manual. She took it out and opened it.

Yes! He'd stuck his vehicle registration inside the front cover. The vehicle was registered to Jake Brand, address 114B George Street in Biloxi. She committed the information to memory, flipped through the manual to be sure no other personal papers were inside, then returned it to the glove box.

A movement caught her attention. He was on his cell phone again, apparently with the same results. He couldn't reach whomever he was so desperate to talk to.

Too antsy to sit still any longer, Lily got out of the car. She wanted to get a good look at the bayou road before the sun went down. She needed to find a landmark that she'd be able to recognize if—no, *when*—she talked to the police.

As she walked toward the warehouse door, Brand stalked toward her, a disapproving frown marring his even features.

"Where the hell do you think you're going?"

"I needed to stretch my legs." She stepped closer to the door to look out. The bayou stretched out before them, and the tangled, overgrown underbrush at the edge of the murky water was deep green. It looked peaceful. There was a sign nailed to a cypress tree. She couldn't make out the words.

"Get away from the door."

"Why? Why are we here?"

Brand didn't answer.

"Are you waiting to turn me over to someone?"

He sent her an exasperated frown. "Just go back to the car."

Lily lifted her chin. "I can't sit in the car doing nothing. If you're going to kill me, why don't you go ahead and do it? It's cruel to make me sit and wait."

He looked down at his feet then out the warehouse door. "I'm not going to kill you, Lily." He shook his head. "I'm trying to save your life. Now will you listen to me and go back to the car?"

Just as he reached for her arm, the distant rumbling of a car engine echoed along the bayou.

He jerked her away from the open doorway and whirled, shoving her against the wall. He flattened his back against the corrugated metal siding beside her. He overlapped her shoulder with his and angled his arm across her middle. The heat from his body seeped into her skin.

"Don't move," he warned her as he slid his handgun from the back of his jeans and cradled it in his left hand.

The car came closer, until the roar of its engine bounced off the metal walls.

Then silence.

Whoever it was, they'd stopped right in front of the warehouse. Lily had never felt so small and helpless in her entire life. She was in the clutches of a dangerous man, and they were being stalked.

Brand pressed Lily back against the wall, her shallow breathing and rapid heartbeat echoing through him. His own pulse hammered as he glanced toward his car. It was dark maroon, which was good. And he'd had sense enough to back it into the warehouse out of the sunlight. However, the door faced west, and the setting sun illuminated the front fender.

Damn it! He'd screwed up. And now, whoever was out there had spotted the car. He had to act fast.

He angled his head and whispered to Lily without taking his eyes off the doorway. "We're going to move toward the back. There's an office on the far wall. If you make a sound, I swear I'll knock you out."

He felt her body stiffen. *Good.* He'd scared her. He hated himself for being so harsh, but it was for her sake, even if she'd never believe it.

He heard two car doors slam. Damn it, there was more than one of them.

He wrapped his arm around Lily's slender waist and guided her through the darkness, praying the rest of the old building was as empty as it had been during his high school days. If they tripped over something, they'd be caught for sure. Brand couldn't let that happen.

They came up against the back wall. Still holding Lily, Brand slid along it until his back rested against a door. His breath whooshed out. He hadn't realized he'd been holding it.

The office. Right where he remembered it. A memory of using the sofa inside for some inept high school groping flashed in his brain. It was gone the next instant, however, as he focused on keeping Lily safe. He felt for the knob and twisted it without turning around.

Relief tightened his throat as the knob turned without resistance. He slid the door open a fraction.

Heavy shoes crunched on gravel and echoed through the building. Two men in uniforms appeared at the open warehouse door.

Police!

Cursing silently, Brand backed through the door to the office and pulled Lily with him. He eased the door shut.

"They're police officers. They can help us," Lily whispered.

"No. Now shut up."

He held her tightly against him, so close he could feel her rapid heartbeats echoing through her frame.

She took a sharp breath. He squeezed her ribs, afraid she

was about to scream. Leaning over, he whispered in her ear. "Do I have to remind you what I said? I will do whatever is necessary to keep you quiet. Do you understand?"

He felt her hair move against his cheek as she nodded. Her entire body trembled.

Loathing leached through him, leaving a bad taste in his mouth. She deserved better than this. In a different world, her delicate beauty and vulnerable mouth would make her just his type.

He even liked her stubborn determination. In fact, he especially liked it—the way she stood up to him, the way her mouth tightened and her chin lifted. The way her brown eyes snapped with irritation.

Brand set his jaw. He couldn't lose himself in thoughts about his lovely hostage. Any lack of focus on his part could get them both killed.

Through the glass-paned door he watched as the officers carefully approached the building, their hands resting on their holstered weapons, their flashlights held at shoulder level. The high-powered beams crossed and swept like spotlights as they scanned the corners and shadows.

Brand eased Lily toward the far side of the tiny office, where he gestured for her to crouch behind the sofa. He hunkered down beside her, waiting, listening, wondering what he would say—what he would do—if the cops found them.

The officers' footsteps were loud in the empty building as they walked around, checking the car and their surroundings.

The footsteps grew closer and closer.

One aimed his flashlight through the glass in the office door, and Brand cringed and held his breath as the beam passed only inches from his foot. He pressed closer to Lily, and rested his left hand against the back of her neck in silent warning.

Tremors shook her slender frame.

"Don't move a muscle," he mouthed in her ear.

She moved her arm. Just as he was about to grab it, she rested her hand on his leg. His thigh muscle jerked.

He swallowed. She was only steadying herself. It wasn't that she trusted him. She didn't. Even if she hadn't said it, he'd seen it in her eyes every time she'd looked at him.

"Hey, Mike. There's an office over here."

Brand raised his gun. It was a futile effort. He could not shoot another officer, even if it meant exposing Lily to danger.

If the officers found them, all he could do was show them his badge and ask to be taken to his lieutenant.

Not that they would agree. Pruitt almost certainly had issued an APB on him by now, and had faxed his name and picture to every police department on the Gulf Coast. If he was caught by the police, he'd be taken into custody in handcuffs and lose his badge.

"Yeah? There's probably a john, too." The second officer's footsteps came closer.

"We ought to check it out."

"Right. Look, I'm ready to get out of here. This place is creepy."

"Creepy?" the first officer repeated with a laugh. "Whoa, Mike. You scared of ghosts?"

"No. If you gotta know, I don't like spiders and there's probably millions of the little monsters in there."

The first officer laughed harder. He swept the interior of the office with his flashlight one more time, aiming the beam at the couch, at the walls, across the floor.

Once again Brand cringed. He shrank back, making his bulk as small as he possibly could. Lily's fingernails dug into his thigh.

"Come on, man, let's go," Mike said. "There's nobody here. We'll call impound. They'll tow the car. Meanwhile we can run the tag, see who pops up. My guess is it's stolen. Some punk kids hid it here until they can sell it."

"Okay, okay. You got the tag number?"

"Yep."

Their voices faded along with their footsteps.

Brand didn't move a muscle until he heard the car start and back out of the driveway.

Then he flopped down on the dirty floor, stretching out his cramped legs in front of him. His breath hissed out through his clenched teeth.

Lily's fingernails were still clamped to his thigh.

Without thinking, he covered her hand with his, running his thumb along her knuckles.

She stiffened.

"It's okay," he whispered, giving her hand a squeeze. "They're gone."

She sat without moving for a long moment. Then she pulled her hand away. "If they run the tag, they'll know who you are, Jake Brand."

He shot her a harsh glance. "You went through the glove box."

She shrugged. "I was bored."

He laughed at her deadpan comment, although inside he acknowledged her statement with a wince.

Yeah, they'd know exactly who he was. A check on the car's registration would reveal that it was a confiscated vehicle signed out to Brandon Gallagher for use in an undercover operation. And in a very short time they'd also know where he was.

"Come on," he said, rising and holding out his hand to her. "We've got to get out of here. They're sending a wrecker for the car."

Lily took his hand and stood, groaning when her leg muscles protested. Her feet had gone numb. She'd sat for too long without moving.

Brand steadied her, his hands under her elbows. She gripped his hard biceps.

His strength called to her in a way she'd never experienced before.

She'd never let herself lean on another person. Her father had taught her to take care of herself, and her ex-husband's lies had reinforced her belief that she could depend on no one but herself.

But now, looking up into Brand's eyes, she realized a terrifying truth. She could lose all her perspective around him.

His intensity and focus, and something about the determined look in his eyes, reminded her of her father.

His brow furrowed and his fingers tightened around hers. His expression held concern and something else she couldn't interpret. His gaze played over her mouth, her throat, her hair. "Are you all right?"

She let go of his arms and backed away. "Yes, I'm fine, for someone who's been threatened and kidnapped, and who's spent the last few minutes hiding from the police."

His intense scrutiny morphed into a frown. "Get in the car." He turned away.

She caught his wrist. "You know, if you would turn yourself in and offer information about Castellano, you could probably get a reduced sentence, or maybe even immunity from prosecution."

He looked down at her hand on his arm, then took it in his. His thumb ran lightly across her knuckles, just like it had when they were hiding. The same odd thrill sang through her, doubling her heart rate.

What was the matter with her? So he was as sexy and appealing as any man she'd ever met. So he had a couple of mannerisms that reminded her of her father. That didn't mean he was anything like Joe Raines. He was a criminal, a fugitive, and she was his hostage.

"You don't understand everything that's going on."

She almost laughed. "You're right about that. Although it's not like I haven't asked. I'm ready to listen if you want to explain everything that's going on to me."

"I can't. Not yet. Just try to believe me when I say I'm doing my best to keep you safe."

She jerked her hand away. "Big of you, since it's your fault I'm in danger. If you're so all-fired concerned about me, why won't you do the one thing I've asked you to do? Let me call the nursing home and check on my father."

He gazed at her for a long moment. Then he pulled out his phone. "What's the number?"

Lily's eyes suddenly stung with tears of relief and joy. "Really? You're going to do it? Oh, my God, I don't have the number. It was in my cell phone, which you destroyed." Her voice broke.

"All right," he sighed. "I'll call directory assistance as soon as we're out of here."

Brand rested his hand at the curve of her hip and carefully eased the office door open. Her heart fluttered like a butterfly in her chest as he guided her back into the dark, empty warehouse.

Despite what he'd put her through, despite the fact that he'd been sent by Castellano to kill her, when he touched her she felt as if she could trust her life to him.

He opened the car's passenger door. "Get in and stay put. I want to be sure everything's clear."

He walked with loose-limbed grace over to the warehouse door. It had grown dark while they'd been hiding from the police. Lily could barely make out his silhouette as he checked out the surrounding area.

Within a few seconds, he was back. He climbed into the car, started the engine and pulled out.

Lily was glad to be out of that warehouse. The officer had been right. It was creepy.

"Where are we going now?"

"I need to check on something," Brand said shortly.

"What about my father?"

He dug out his cell phone.

Lily reached for it, but he held it away from her.

"I'll do the calling."

He dialed three digits without looking at the buttons. After a few seconds he spoke. "Beachside Manor, Biloxi. Yes, go ahead and dial it."

He listened, then handed her the phone.

"May I help you?" the voice asked.

"The nurses' station on the Blue Wing, please."

"Please hold."

Lily clutched the cell phone like a lifeline.

Dear God, please let Dad be all right. She tried to pay attention to the streets Brand took, but she was too anxious to find out about her father.

"Blue Wing. Starling." It was the Blue Wing's supervisory nurse.

"Ms. Starling. It's Lily Raines." Her pulse raced and fear and anticipation clogged her throat.

"Oh, hi, Ms. Raines. I've been trying to reach you."

Lily's heart seized. "Why? Is everything okay? My father?"

"Oh yes, everything is fine. But I am glad you called. I left a message on your home phone earlier today. We've been concerned about that gentleman who was supposed to pick up your father. The poor man who was mugged and killed on the way here."

"I know. It was awful." She glanced over at Brand, who appeared to be concentrating on his driving.

"I wanted to ask you if you had sent someone else to pick him up."

Panic lodged in Lily's throat. "No!" she rasped. "No! You haven't let anyone see him have you?"

"No, ma'am. A man came by earlier this afternoon. He seemed nice enough at first, but when I explained to him that he couldn't see your father without your permission, he became rude and demanding. I had to call the security guard before he finally gave up and went away."

"Who was it?"

"He wouldn't give his name. That's why I called security."

Lily's hands shook so badly she almost dropped the phone. She thought about the fire in her dad's wastebasket.

Castellano's men had gotten to him once. They could again.

"Please make sure no one gets in to see him. No one but me."

"Of course, Ms. Raines. Will you be coming by soon?"

She looked at Brand. "As soon as I possibly can."

"Ms. Raines, are you all right?"

Lily swallowed and tried to make her voice sound normal. "I'm fine. Thank you for letting me know about the man." She fumbled with the disconnect button, her fingers numb with fear.

Brand gently took the phone from her and pocketed it. "What's the matter? Did someone try to get to your father?"

She glared at him. "You should know. Isn't that the plan, to threaten my father? He was sent by Castellano." She took a shaky breath. "You have to take me there. I have to make sure he's safe."

He knew she was right. If it had been the police who'd shown up at the nursing home, they wouldn't have hesitated to flash their badges.

His fists clenched on the steering wheel, his chest tightening with foreboding. Why hadn't Pruitt picked up her father and put him in protective custody? What the hell was Pruitt's problem? That made it three times the FBI agent had let him down.

He vowed to call him as soon as he could manage it without Lily overhearing. He'd demand to know what was going on.

"Answer me!" Lily shouted.

"I can't take you there. The nursing home is being watched."

"Castellano sent someone to kill my father." Her voice was shrill. She was about to fall apart.

Brand nodded, working to keep his expression bland. *Damn it.* It wouldn't take Castellano long to figure out a way to get to Joe Raines. He'd managed it once already. That fire in the wastebasket hadn't been an accident.

"Please. Dear God, please take me to him."

"No. That's not going to happen." Brand stopped at a stop sign and turned to Lily. He covered her hand where it rested on her knee. She tried to pull away, but he wrapped his fingers around hers and held on tight.

"Listen to me. The police will pick up your father and place him in protective custody. They should do that any time now."

"How do you know?"

He shrugged. "You were a juror on a high-profile murder case. Now you're missing. A former police officer was killed on his way to Beachside Manor. The police aren't dumb. They'll be right on top of Henderson's killing and it won't take them long to put two and two together.

As soon as they do, they'll get your father out of there." He squeezed her hand. "He'll be transported to a secure facility. He'll be safe."

A sob escaped her throat. "Safe."

He knew what she was thinking. Her father's safety was the most important thing, but she had no idea if Brand were telling the truth or not. She didn't trust him, and he couldn't blame her.

He'd done little to earn her trust.

He turned his attention back to the road. They were approaching his lieutenant's street. It worried him that he hadn't been able to get in touch with Morrison.

From the time Brand first joined the force, Morrison had taken him under his wing. He'd been more like a father to him than his own father ever had. Morrison was the one man Brand could trust.

So why was he suddenly unreachable?

As he approached the corner, he saw a car turn onto Morrison's street. His senses went on red alert. The vehicle passed under a streetlight, and he recognized the glint of a portable police light on the dashboard.

What the hell? A glimpse of a broad, florid face inside the car told him the driver wasn't Morrison. Brand slowed and looked down the street. There were at least three unmarked vehicles parked along the curb.

Cops. He knew it in his gut. He cursed under his breath.

Had something happened to Morrison, or were they waiting for him?

He sped up and away. He didn't know if any of the cars had spotted him, but he wasn't taking any chances.

"What's the matter?"

He arched his shoulders to relieve the tension. "Nothing."

"That's not true. You saw something."

He grimaced inwardly. She was perceptive. "Nothing you need to be concerned about."

"I disagree. I'm concerned about everything you do, since you're holding me hostage."

Brand studied her. Then he asked the question that had been gnawing at his gut. "Why didn't you scream for help when the officers showed up at the warehouse?"

She stared at him in surprise. Her mouth opened, but nothing came out. She pressed her lips together and looked down at her hands. "I'm not sure."

"Could it be that you don't trust the police, either?"

"Of course I trust the police. My father was on the force for over twenty years."

Her wide brown eyes met his, and he saw confusion and wariness in their unfathomable depths.

"So? You could be in police custody now, where you'd feel safe. Why didn't you scream?"

She pressed her lips together and looked down at her hands. "I should have, but—"

"But?" Had she thought he would kill her?

"I was afraid they'd shoot you."

Chapter Six

Her answer stunned him. She was afraid for his life?

Her head was still down and her profile was silhouetted against the glow from the streetlights. Her nose turned up slightly, her brows arched delicately over her eyes, and as he watched, that stubborn chin lifted.

"Odd behavior from a cop's daughter."

She angled her head to stare at him. "So you think I should have screamed for the police?"

"No. I'm grateful you didn't." He took a right turn, keeping an eye on the traffic. He had no idea where to go. Maybe he should drive east, toward Pascagoula, and look for a hotel.

"I should have," she repeated.

His cell phone rang. Surprised, he checked the caller ID. *Pruitt.* Damn it.

He pulled into a dark side street and stopped. He wasn't about to chance Lily overhearing the FBI agent on the phone. In one motion he turned off the car and opened the door.

"Stay put," he told Lily, then slammed the car door.

"Yeah?" he grated through clenched teeth as he walked a few steps away from the vehicle.

"Gallagher, what the hell are you doing?"

"What am I doing? Don't give me that!" He kept his eye on Lily as he walked farther away. "What the hell are *you* doing? Where were your arresting officers, man? I thought you were going to pick up Foshee and me at the courthouse."

"There's a bigger issue at stake here."

"A bigger issue than Lily Raines's life?"

"Listen to me, Gallagher, and drop the attitude. I got word from Carson there's a very important shipment coming in. He thinks it may be automatic weapons."

"What does that have to do with you hanging me out to dry?"

"We've got to stay under the radar. We don't want anything to jeopardize this shipment. If we had picked up Foshee, Castellano would be alerted, and we'd lose our chance."

"Well, I beat up Foshee to keep him from killing Lily. So what do you think Castellano thinks about me?"

"We're hoping he'll think you're a loose cannon—which you are! Look, Gallagher. If we can nail 'em with the smuggled weapons in their hands, then we can put Castellano away for good. That's all you need to know. Now where the hell are you and what the hell are you doing? I assume you have the juror."

"I can't tell you where I am right now, and I'm about to hang up, so don't even think about triangulating on the cell phone signal. There's something fishy going on. I can't let anyone know where I am until I figure out what it is."

"I'm giving you a direct order. If you don't come in immediately, I'll suspend you."

"No problem, *boss*. Being suspended is the least of

my worries right now." He glanced over his shoulder at the car. Lily was watching him. He started back toward the vehicle.

"Why haven't you picked up Joe Raines?"

"The old man? You gonna bring the girl in so we can get her signed permission?"

Brand kept silent.

"That's what I thought. So we have to get a court order to remove him from the nursing home. These things take time."

"Well, rush it. Castellano's already gotten to him once, and he tried again today. Call me when he's safe."

"Gallagher, are you really gonna lose your badge over a girl?"

Brand hung up and headed back to the car. He was certain Pruitt had all available squad cars on the lookout for them. He had to find a place where they could hide. He'd ditch the car as soon as he could.

Lily saw the anger and frustration on Brand's face as he got in and started the engine without speaking.

"What was that about?"

He made a U-turn and pulled out of the side street. "Nothing."

"It didn't look like nothing." She studied his grim face. "I keep trying to figure out what you're planning to do with me. You're waiting for instructions, aren't you? Is it Castellano? Is that who you're supposed to turn me over to?" She swallowed hard. The idea had been growing in her mind ever since he'd rescued her from Foshee.

He sent her a dark look. "I'm not turning you over to Castellano. Haven't you figured that out by now?"

Lily's frustration boiled over. "Well, excuse me. I was abducted and handcuffed and thrown into a stranger's car. Forgive me if I can't quite *keep up* with what you're thinking." She crossed her arms and pushed back in her seat, watching him out of the corner of her eye.

He shot her an amused glance, ramping up her anger. She turned away and looked out the window.

After a few moments of driving in silence, he turned east.

Lily found herself watching him again. His hands were white-knuckled on the steering wheel. His wide, straight mouth was set, and a tiny frown furrowed the space between his brows.

"You don't look like a thug."

His brows shot up and his mouth quirked upward. He was smiling.

"Thank you, I reckon," he said wryly.

"I mean it. You're not slimy like the Cajun, nor too slick like Sack Simon. How did you end up working for Castellano?"

"I guess I'm just a lucky guy."

His jaw flexed again and the half smile was gone. Lily clung to her mistrust of him like a starving man holding tight to his last morsel of food. She couldn't afford to be influenced by a pair of kind blue eyes or a strong, determined jaw.

"Come on. Nobody wakes up one morning when they're a kid and says 'I want to be an enforcer for an organized crime boss.'"

"That's true."

He glanced in the rearview mirror, and the furrow appeared between his brows again.

"What is it?"

"I'm not sure. We may have picked up a tail."

Lily turned to look behind her. She saw a couple of cars, but neither one of them were close. "How can you tell?"

"So, Lily. What did you want to be when you grew up?"

"What?" She was surprised. Was he trying to distract her from the vehicle following them?

"A nurse? A teacher? Miss America?"

Despite her worry, she laughed. "I suppose like any child, I wanted to be just like my father. I wanted to be a cop."

Brand cut his eyes up to the rearview mirror again.

"What about you?" she asked.

His lips pressed together for an instant. "I wanted to be anything *but* just like my dad. Hold on."

He took a sharp left in front of a black SUV.

Lily cried out and grabbed for the armrest as the massive vehicle missed the rear of Brand's car by mere inches. Its horn blared.

She jumped. "What are you doing?"

"Losing the tail I hope." He straightened the vehicle and raced down the side street.

Lily turned around in her seat. "Is it the police?"

"More likely Castellano's men."

"How did they find us?"

"They know my car."

Lily saw the dark car turn onto the street behind them. "There they are. They're following us."

Brand whipped the car to the right, down an alley between two restaurants.

Lily's heart jumped into her throat. "Where are you going?"

"Cutting through to a major street. Trying to lose them."

All at once, a wall of rusted metal loomed in front of them.

"Look out!" she cried, automatically raising her arms to shield her face.

It was a metal garbage Dumpster, and it blocked the alley. Brand slammed on the brakes and whipped the car sideways. The tires screeched. The car halted less than two feet from the dirty metal container.

"Damn it!" He slapped the steering wheel with his palm. The garbage truck had set the Dumpster down right in the middle of the alley. There was no room for a car to pass.

He cut the engine and turned off the lights. Shifting in his seat, he kept watch on the narrow alley through which they'd come. "Go around the Dumpster. There'll be a door on your left. Go straight through the kitchen, find the bathroom and stay there until I come and get you."

Lily grabbed his arm. "What about you?"

"I'm going to get these guys off our tail. Now run."

"Not without you."

He shook his head. "Too dangerous. If I do that I'll be leading them into a restaurant full of people. I've got to stop them out here."

"But what if you can't—"

Brand covered her hand with his. "Then you call the police." He squeezed her hand. "Run."

She got out of the car and ran toward the Dumpster. She

slipped around it just as the black car passed the alley. Brand had no time to even breathe before the car backed up and turned into the alley.

Cursing under his breath, he slid out of the driver's seat and crouched behind the car, using it as a shield. With calm efficiency he drew his weapon and checked it, making sure he had a full magazine.

The dark car stopped a few feet away from his rear bumper. Both doors opened and two men jumped out, using the open car doors as shields.

"Hey, *bioque*." It was Foshee. His voice was more nasal than usual.

Brand trained his weapon on the passenger door, where a narrow strip of white bobbed up and down in the shadows.

"You broke my nose. You gonna pay for that." Foshee let loose a string of nasty curses in French.

Brand laughed without humor. The strip of white was a bandage on Foshee's large nose.

The other man, the driver, yelled at Brand. "Where's the girl?"

"Gone. I don't have her."

"You're a lying pig. You got her there somewhere. Give her up and we'll let you live."

"Yeah. Long enough to deliver me to Castellano."

Foshee's head popped up from behind the car door and a shot zinged past Brand's head.

He fired back, aiming for the window. It shattered. Then he shifted his aim and shot the driver's window out.

"Get out of here, Foshee. I don't want to have to kill you."

The Cajun laughed. "It's two against one, Brand. You got no chance."

Brand eyed the shoes that stuck out beneath the car door. "Sounds like pretty good odds to me."

Foshee fired, and the bullet screeched along the top of Brand's car. He ducked, feeling a sliver of metal prick his cheek. After a couple of seconds he rose and fired off two rounds at Foshee's feet.

The Cajun screamed and dove back into the car.

The driver's side of the car was angled slightly away from his line of sight, so he couldn't get a bead on the driver's feet. He fired anyway, trying to aim through the shattered window.

The last thing he wanted to do was kill someone, but Lily was inside the restaurant waiting for him, depending on him to protect her from Castellano. He'd do what he had to.

The driver fired back. The metallic thud of the bullet hitting the side of the car rang in Brand's ears. Then he heard something else.

Sirens. Getting louder.

Were they responding to the gunshots? Equal parts of relief and apprehension coursed through him.

A muffled groan and shadowy movement in the car's interior told him Foshee was still conscious. Brand fired again at each door, then took careful aim and shot out the vehicle's two front tires.

The police sirens kept coming, getting louder. As a squad car sped past the alley and its brake lights flashed, Brand turned and skirted the Dumpster and burst into the restaurant's kitchen.

The odors of grease, fish and fresh bread wafted around him as he plowed through the service area, ignoring the shocked looks and exclamations of the staff. He headed for the women's bathroom.

He flung open the door and crossed the lounge in two long strides. As his pulse raced with apprehension, he stuck his head in the bathroom door.

"Lily?"

He heard a muffled sob. The sound froze his heart. With his weapon clutched in both hands, he slipped through the door.

There, at the far end of the tiled room, a man in a dark suit with a fighter's flattened nose held a gun to Lily's head. His other arm was wrapped around her neck.

She stood stiffly, her eyes sparkling with tears as she met Brand's gaze.

"I'm sorry," she whispered.

"Shut up!" The man pushed the gun into her temple and tightened his arm.

She coughed.

"You coward," Brand taunted. "Hiding behind a woman. How the hell did you get in here, anyhow?"

The thug grinned. "When you pulled into this alley, there was only two ways you could go. Through the alley on foot, or into the restaurant. There's a guy at the other end of the alley, too."

Brand wanted to shoot the sneering grin off the man's face. "Let her go. She's got nothing to do with this. Shoot me."

"It ain't you he wants. You I can take care of right here with one shot."

"Yeah? Go ahead. Shoot me, but I'll guarantee I'll drop you before I die."

A muffled cry escaped Lily's lips and tears slipped down her cheeks.

Brand moved closer.

"Don't try it," the thug warned.

But Brand only had one chance, and he was betting it all on Castellano giving orders to have Lily brought to him alive. The thug couldn't kill her, so he had to kill Brand.

He sent Lily a quick look, hoping beyond hope that she could read his intent. She was a cop's daughter. Surely her father had taught her how to defend herself.

She clasped her fingers together in front of her in a pleading gesture. "I'll go with you. Just don't hurt him, please," she begged the man holding her.

The thug took his gun away from her temple and aimed it at Brand. "Sorry, sweetheart," he laughed. "But I've got my orders. Besides, I'm going to enjoy this."

Lily used the force of her left hand against her right fist to drive her elbow into his midsection.

"Oof!" He doubled over. His finger reflexively pulled the trigger but his shot went wild. Lily broke away and backed up against the wall.

At the same time, Brand hit the floor and rolled. He knocked the guy's two-hundred-dollar shoes out from under him. The big man collapsed with a loud thud and his gun skidded across the slick tile floor and clanged against the far wall.

Brand came up onto his knees. He aimed his gun right at the guy's heart.

But the thug just groaned and tried to push himself up. A knot was already swelling on his sweaty forehead where he'd hit the floor.

Brand stood and placed a foot on the man's burly neck and pulled a Flexicuff out of his jeans. He cuffed the man's hands behind his back. Then he grabbed a couple of paper towels and stuffed them in his mouth. With one foot, he shoved him under the door of the closest stall.

"Come on."

Lily turned toward him, stopping just short of flinging herself into his arms. Her wide brown eyes were huge in her pale face and the tracks of tears glistened on her cheeks. She quickly gave him the once-over.

"Are you hurt? Did he hit you?" she asked shakily.

He shook his head. "What about you?"

She shook her head. "I'm fine."

But Brand could tell that she wasn't. Her hands were shaking. Her eyes still held a haunted fear.

"That was a good move. Your dad teach you that?"

She nodded jerkily. "I never did it for real before."

"Well, you did good." He gave her a little smile. "You're tougher than you look. Let's get out of here. We don't have much time. It's not going to take long for somebody to figure out that those were gunshots."

"Shouldn't we get his gun?"

Just as she spoke the lounge door opened and an older woman entered. She gasped. "Oh, my word! What is going on here?"

Brand took Lily's arm and squeezed it. "Nothing, ma'am. I was worried about my wife. But she's fine."

He surreptitiously tucked his gun into his belt and guided Lily past the woman and out the door. They turned right, toward the main exit.

Behind them, a scream loud enough to be heard over the music erupted from the women's bathroom.

"Help! There's a dead man in here!"

The door from the kitchen burst open. Lily looked over her shoulder. She went rigid.

"It's the police," she whispered.

Brand's heart hammered. He kept his head down. "Don't look at them. Keep walking."

They were almost at the exit. Another three seconds and they'd be out of there.

"But they could help us." Lily half turned, but Brand held on to her arm as the woman from the bathroom emerged, screaming, "It's them! They're getting away!"

People began to stir and whisper. A waiter started toward them.

"Walk," he commanded.

Once they were outside, he looked up and down the street. "Come on. This way." He headed east.

Lily was forced to half run to keep up with him. "I don't understand. Castellano's men are trying to kill you. Why won't you let the police help?"

"I've seen things that make me worry that some of the police are in Castellano's pocket."

"That can't be true."

Brand stopped. "Whether you believe it or not, it can be true. And if I trust the wrong person, you may not escape Castellano's clutches next time."

Her shoulders hunched and he watched a shiver ripple through her.

He stole a glance back at the restaurant they'd just left. Then he pointed ahead of them. "See the hotel up there? We'll cut through there and grab a cab on the other side, the Carroll Street entrance."

He pulled her with him to the building side of the sidewalk, staying out of the line of sight of the police when they came out of the restaurant.

As they reached the hotel, he risked another glance backward. Sure enough, two police officers ran out of the restaurant, looking up and down the street.

Brand wrapped his arm around Lily's neck like a lover and urged her forward, wincing when a breeze lifted her hair and blew it across his face.

The smell of fresh coconut and vanilla reminded him of how soft and vulnerable her neck had been when he'd bandaged it. How close he'd been to her lips, close enough to see them quiver.

He groaned silently as he followed her through the hotel lobby door.

"Keep walking," he said, pushing her ahead of him and dropping back a few steps. He pulled out his cell phone and dialed a familiar number. When his brother answered, Brand breathed a sigh of relief.

"Ry, it's me. Can I ask a favor of you?"

"I can barely hear you. What is it? I'm on my way to bed."

The impatience in Ryan's voice made Brand sad. He'd always looked up to his older brother, always counted on him. But ever since he'd gone undercover, they'd grown apart.

He put his mouth right against the phone, making sure Lily couldn't hear him. "You said Cassie wasn't using her studio?"

"That's right. Hasn't since she found out she was pregnant. Turpentine, mineral spirits—all that can be bad for the baby."

"Can I borrow it? Just for a day or two."

"What kind of jam have you gotten yourself into this time, kid?"

"I'm, uh—protecting a witness. Come on, Ry. I'm in a hurry. I need a place to hide out where no one would think to look for me."

Ryan sighed. "Does this have to do with Castellano?"

"Kind of."

Ryan cursed. "I don't like it."

"It's just a couple of days. Ry, it's a matter of life and death."

"Get serious, Brand."

"I *am* serious. I've got a witness who can bring Castellano down."

Ryan was silent.

"Thanks, bud. I won't touch a thing. I promise."

"Brand, how much trouble are you in?"

"Not too much."

"Damn it, Brand. How do you let yourself get sucked into these situations?"

Ahead of him, Lily had reached the Carroll Street entrance. She turned and sent him a questioning glance, her face drawn and white. His heart squeezed in sympathy. She was so tired and so scared. No matter how brave she acted, she'd almost died back there, and she knew it.

He hated being the reason her brown eyes were dull and the spark he'd admired was gone. She wouldn't make it much further without rest.

He considered Ryan's question. How had he gotten sucked into this situation? How could he not? He couldn't let Foshee kill her. He turned his attention back to his brother. "I've always had a flair for excitement," he said wryly.

"Yeah, I'd say so. So who's the witness you're protecting?"

"You know I can't tell you that. Is there a key somewhere, so I can get into the studio without having to break in?"

Ryan sighed. "Look in the mailbox. Cassie keeps a spare key there. I've warned her about it, but for some reason she thinks nobody can figure that out."

Brand smiled. "You tell her thanks."

"I'd just as soon not tell her anything. See that you don't mess up the place, okay?"

Brand grunted. Messing up the place was the least of his worries. "Ry, how's Mom?"

"She's doing okay. She's having a ball with the baby."

"That's good. Would you tell her something for me? Tell her I'll see her as soon as I can."

"Yeah. I'll tell her. Take care of yourself, kid."

A pricking behind his eyes surprised him. When did he get so damned sentimental about family?

"I will, Ry. Thanks."

He disconnected and glanced over his shoulder. So far the police hadn't gotten to the hotel.

He guided Lily to the lobby door. "Wait here until I get a taxi."

Lily nodded. As soon as Brand's hand left her back, she

reached out to steady herself against the wall. She was so tired she could barely stand and so spooked she couldn't think. She'd never been so close to death. She could still feel the cold steel of the gun's barrel pressed into her temple, still smell the cigarette smoke on the man's breath.

Suddenly, her stomach churned. Now that it was all over, she couldn't believe she'd had sense enough to use her elbow like her father had taught her. She couldn't believe the move had worked. All she could do was shake her head in wonder. She'd helped, but Brand had saved her again.

He'd saved her. She had no idea who he was, no clue what his motives were. But his strong arms around her made her feel as if nothing bad could happen to her. His intense blue eyes promised her safety. And if she looked closely enough, she could imagine that they promised something else. Something baser, sweeter than security.

An electric spark of desire ignited deep within her. She gasped quietly, then blew air out through her pursed lips. She couldn't think that way. She couldn't *feel* that way.

She wasn't thinking clearly, that was all. She hadn't had a decent night's sleep since Brand and the Cajun had threatened her and her father the first time, and today she'd been close to death three times. She felt numb and terrified at the same time—an odd combination.

Brand spoke quickly with the doorman, who made a call on his cell phone. Then he stepped back inside the door, filling her senses with the aura of confidence and strong sexiness that surrounded him.

"The taxi will be here in a few minutes," he said. "Stay back, away from the door."

She nodded jerkily. She hadn't forgotten how dangerous their situation was.

"Are you all right?" he asked, taking her arm.

"Sure. I'm fine."

"We'll be somewhere safe in ten minutes."

"Somewhere safe?" Dear God, if she could only believe that. A laugh that felt faintly hysterical bubbled up from her chest. "Are you kidding me? The only safe place I can think of is the one place you won't go." She put up a shaky hand to tuck her hair behind her ear.

"The police? I told you I can't afford to do that. Not yet."

Helpless frustration swept through her, along with apprehension. What if Brand was playing her for a fool until he could get her to Castellano? What if she were blinded by the kindness she glimpsed in his eyes when he looked at her?

To her dismay, her eyes filled with tears. "Well, when then? How many times do we have to be chased and shot at before you turn yourself in?"

The taxi appeared.

"Turn myself in?" His voice held a hard edge.

"You're running from Castellano and running from the law. That tells me you've done something really bad."

"Does it?" He scowled at her, his expression hard. "Our ride's here. Let's go."

The doorman held the door and Brand guided her quickly to the vehicle. He deposited her in the backseat then climbed in after her.

"Three eleven Woodmont," he told the driver. "In Pass Christian."

The taxi pulled out and made a U-turn.

Lily sat back in the seat and sighed. She longed to close her burning eyes, but she found herself watching Brand.

He scanned the sidewalks and the oncoming traffic as well as the cars behind them. His hand rested lightly on her knee, and his shoulder pressed against hers.

She shook her head, trying to dislodge the dangerous notion that he wasn't a threat. She was beginning to think of him as some sort of hero. She'd be hallucinating in a minute.

She tilted her head and examined his profile. She knew appearances could be deceiving. Knew better than to trust someone just because they looked like a nice person. She'd trusted her ex-husband and look where that had gotten her.

But all her careful caution and her meager experience with men didn't stop her from trusting Brand. She trusted him even though she knew how dangerous that could be. Because he had to be one of two things—an enforcer for Castellano, or some kind of vigilante.

A third possibility tickled the edge of her mind. She rejected it immediately. There was no way he was a cop. Not with his obvious disdain for the police. Unless—

Her pulse sped up and her mouth went dry as she realized his attitude could have another root cause. And if that was the case, she was in a lot more trouble than she'd first thought.

Her father had always said that there was nothing more dangerous than a rogue cop.

Chapter Seven

The place where Brand had brought them was an old building, subdivided into offices. As he retrieved a key from the mailbox, Lily tried to read the name on the box's label. It looked like *Galloway* or *Gallagher*—she couldn't quite tell. She only got a brief glimpse.

They went up to the second floor and Brand unlocked the door to what appeared to be a small studio. The first thing that hit Lily was the smell of turpentine. She stepped inside, around a roll of canvas and a box of paint tubes.

An easel stood near the window, with a stool in front of it. An artist's palette, covered with globs of bright paint, lay on the stool. There were canvases stacked everywhere—against the walls and on the floor. On her left a bedraggled daybed was piled high with sketches and books.

"Whose studio is this?"

Brand turned from locking the dead bolt. "I can't answer that."

"Of course not." Lily sighed. "I don't understand why you don't trust me." She flung her arms out. "Who am I going to tell?"

"You're safer not knowing anything. Then you won't have to lie."

"Lie? Why would I lie?"

"Don't worry about it. It doesn't matter anyhow." He pocketed the keys and stepped past her, his shoulder brushing hers. That ridiculous spark of yearning streaked through her again, weakening her knees and shocking her senses. How was she going to fight this absurd attraction to the man who had taken her hostage?

The man who'd saved her.

Her heart sped up in a staccato rhythm as she tried to deny the sudden thrill that flowed from her loins all the way out to her fingers and toes.

She was *not* attracted to him, she told herself sternly. She couldn't be. He wasn't one of the good guys.

He crossed the tiny room and peered through the edge of the closed blinds. "We can see the street from here. That's good. As long as we keep watch, nobody can sneak up on us."

He surveyed the room. "That door leads to the bathroom. There's a window in there, but I wouldn't advise climbing out. It's a long drop to the ground."

Lily smiled grimly. "No problem. But if you don't mind—" She gestured toward the door.

"Go ahead." Brand stepped aside.

Lily eased past him and slipped into the minuscule bathroom. Closing the door behind her, she leaned against it for a few seconds as tears stung her eyes and a sob escaped her lips.

It was all too much. Had it really been just this afternoon that she'd sat in the courtroom with eleven other jurors and returned a guilty verdict? Had it been no more than a few hours ago that Brand had held her at knifepoint, then turned the tables and rescued her from Foshee?

She peered in the tiny mirror and fingered the awkward bandage on her neck. Peeling off the tape, she tilted her head to look at the cut. It wasn't deep but it was almost two inches long. Two inches. That's how close she'd come to dying.

She turned on the water and splashed it on her face. The cool liquid soothed her burning eyes and helped to clear her head.

A couple of towels were folded on the back of the toilet and a bottle of floral-scented hand soap sat next to the sink. At least she'd figured out one thing. The owner of the studio was a woman. She quickly splashed her face one more time, then used one of the towels to dry off.

When she opened the bathroom door, Brand was gathering up a stack of sketches from the daybed.

He had to move out of the way before the door would open fully. Lily slipped past him and went over to the easel. "She's good."

"Who?"

"Whoever painted these. Is it your girlfriend?" She picked up one of the canvases stacked against the wall and held it up. It was a portrait of a child, done in a soft, impressionistic style.

He looked up from turning down the covers. "No. Leave them alone."

She set the portrait down and turned another canvas around. It depicted a bowl of apples sitting on the windowsill. "They're really lovely."

"Come away from the window," he said irritably. "You can sleep here. I'll keep watch."

"All night? You can't do that."

"Just try to sleep."

Lily slipped out of her heels and her suit jacket and lay down. She relaxed into the too-soft mattress of the daybed. Her shoulders and neck ached, her feet hurt and she didn't think she'd ever been so tired in her life.

Brand turned out the lights, but a glaring yellow glow from a gas station across the street filtered through the blinds, casting long, striped shadows on the floor.

He stood beside the window, peered out through the edge of the blinds and started unbuttoning his shirt.

Lily watched him in stunned silence. She could hardly breathe as he shrugged out of the dress shirt.

He tossed it on a stack of canvases. The white T-shirt underneath stretched over his broad shoulders and across his tight middle. His arms were corded with long, sleek muscles.

The light from the window threw him into silhouette, emphasizing the clean planes of his face and body. With his arms bare, he looked less bulky, less formidable, though not a bit less sexy.

He pulled his weapon out of his waistband and checked it thoroughly before placing it on top of his shirt. Then he went back to keeping watch.

Lily fought the desire that arrowed through her. Despite her efforts, her thighs tightened and her pulse pounded. She decided Brand was the sexiest man she'd ever known.

Her eyes traced the strong curve of his back, the sleek line of his shoulders. His profile was classic, marred only by a slightly crooked nose. His mouth was straight, his jaw strong. He looked like a warrior silhouetted against the night sky.

Her pulse pounded and a strange ache began in the region of her heart. What would it be like to be loved by him? To make love with someone that intense, someone that strong?

She clenched her fists. She had to stop thinking about him in that way. She had to concentrate on getting to the police.

"Do you think they'll find us?"

He angled his head without taking his gaze from the street outside. "Not unless—" He stopped. "No."

Lily sat up and hugged a throw pillow. "Not unless what?"

"Nothing. Go to sleep."

"What are you waiting for? Are you supposed to hear from somebody? Is that who you keep trying to call?"

He didn't answer.

"You could just drop me off at police headquarters. I know a lot of the officers. They'll protect me. I promise I wouldn't say anything about you."

"You promise?" He laughed. "That makes me feel better."

"So you're holding me to protect yourself? It doesn't look like it's working very well. I'd think you'd do better without me."

"Listen to me, Lily. Whether you choose to believe me or not, your life is in danger. And trust me, going to the police is no guarantee of safety."

"Why do you keep saying that?" His dogged certainty planted a seed of doubt in her breast. She did her best to ignore it. "I grew up around the police. My father was a police officer. His fellow officers, his friends, will take care of me. That's what police officers do. They take care of their own. They'll put me in protective custody until Castellano is caught."

"Yeah? And what if one of those officers you think you know so well is actually working for Castellano? What then?"

"That won't happen."

"It already has."

"You know that for a fact?"

He nodded. "I just don't know who."

His cell phone rang, startling her.

Brand dug the phone out of his pocket and looked at the caller ID. It was Pruitt again. He pressed the disconnect button, rejecting the call.

Lily turned onto her side. Her eyes glittered in the faint light from the blinds. "I'm really tired."

"I know," he said softly. "Why don't you get some sleep?"

"I'm not sure I can. It's been a rough day."

"Yeah."

"Talk to me," she murmured.

Brand's gaze followed the sleek line of her neck, the curve of her hip, her long, shapely legs. "About what?" he asked, hearing the rasp of yearning in his voice.

"Anything, I don't care. Just talk."

He thought about her growing up with a police officer for a father. How reassuring that must have been for a child to know that her dad was a good man.

"Was your dad always a cop?"

She nodded. "Ever since I can remember. He was the strongest, most honest man I've ever known."

Brand's heart ached. The closest he'd ever had to a father like that was his older brother. But Ryan had never approved of him becoming a cop. Then when Brand had taken the undercover assignment to bring down Castellano, Ryan had accused him of seeking revenge for Patrick's murder.

Brand had never admitted to Ryan that revenge on Castellano was always in the back of his mind. Revenge wasn't a heroic purpose. But then he'd never claimed to be a hero. Still, he'd like to think he was bringing Castellano down because it was the right thing to do. The crime boss had hurt too many people, including Lily.

He looked up to find her sleepy gaze on him.

"What about your mother?" he asked her.

"She died when I was twelve. My dad reared me on his own."

"No brothers and sisters?"

"No. Just me and my dad."

"Is your ex-husband a cop?"

"No. He's a prominent real-estate lawyer. I can't even remember why I married him. And trust me, I will never forget why I divorced him."

"Why did you?"

She sighed. "The usual reason I suppose. He cheated on me." Her shoulders moved in a slight shrug. "And he hated that I had my own career. He tried to stop me from working, tried to control every aspect of my life."

Brand knew the type. He'd worked his share of domestic disturbances. How could anyone married to a woman like Lily mistreat or cheat on her? His heart squeezed painfully. She was beautiful, kind, gutsy. And sexy as hell. Everything a man could want in a woman.

Impotent anger at the jerk who'd treated her badly swelled inside him. If she'd stayed in the marriage, she could have ended up hurt or dead. A sudden urge overwhelmed him. He wanted to gather her into his arms and show her what a man who didn't hate women could give her.

Quickly, he changed the direction of his thoughts.

"So what do you do, Lily?"

"I'm an interior designer. But what about you, Jake Brand? Are you married?"

He laughed shortly. She'd turned the tables on him. He should have seen that coming. He shook his head. "Not even close."

"What about your parents? Brothers and sisters?"

"My father just died."

"I'm sorry."

"Don't be. He was an alcoholic. Made my mother's life a living hell."

"Your poor mother. That's so sad. Is that why you said you'd rather be anything other than like your father?"

Brand didn't answer. Couldn't. He never talked about his family to anyone. It surprised the hell out of him that he'd said so much to Lily.

"You were going to tell me how you ended up working for Castellano."

"Was I?"

She smiled. "I need to know."

"No, you don't. Like I told you, the less you know, the safer you'll be."

"You actually believe the police are the bad guys, don't you?"

He looked out the window. "Not all of them. Just certain ones."

"You shouldn't judge everyone based on what one person did to you."

He grimaced at her words. He'd lived his life believing all families were as dysfunctional as his. That all fathers drank and yelled and hit. That everyone's mother cried and cowered in the corner.

In his experience family and what passed for love were inextricably bound in pain and fear.

Lily would never understand how his life had been shaped by what his father had done to his mother, to his brothers and him. She'd had a good father and a decent, loving family.

She yawned. "I can't stay awake."

"You don't have to. I'm here. I'll take care of you."

He sat still, listening to her quiet breaths until they turned soft and even. She was asleep.

Brand walked over and pulled the covers up to her shoulders.

She smiled and said something he didn't catch.

"Sleep tight, Lily," he whispered. An impulse he couldn't explain made him lean over and kiss her cheek. Her soft scent enveloped him and her hair tickled his nose.

He pulled back and studied her face, her hair, the red scratch on her neck where he'd cut her. He frowned and reached out a hand, but stopped short of touching her.

He wasn't quite sure what made her so appealing. She was pretty, with dark brown eyes and hair and a fair complexion. Her slim body was nice enough.

She was pleasant to look at, but nothing special. Except

that when all of it came together—when her eyes snapped with interest or irritation and her teeth scraped gently across her vulnerable lower lip, he had to struggle to maintain control of his body.

Ever since the first time he'd seen her, while he'd held her for Foshee to threaten, he'd been attracted to her.

He touched her hair. "I'm sorry you got mixed up in this, Lily. I'm doing my best to protect you."

Turning away, he searched in the dark until he found Cassie's phone book in a desk drawer. He looked up his lieutenant's home phone number and punched it into his cell phone. Then he unlocked the dead bolt and slipped out into the hall.

He pressed the call button. The phone rang and rang.

"Damn it, Morrison." Brand scowled. What was going on? Had something happened to the lieutenant?

Finally someone picked up. "Yeah?" a gruff voice said.

"Morrison? It's Gallagher."

He heard a low groan and the sharp creak of bedsprings. "Hang on," Morrison whispered.

Brand paced back and forth, grazing his knuckles with his teeth. Through the phone he heard rustling and the sound of a door closing softly.

Then the lieutenant was back. "Brand. Where the hell are you? What's the matter with you? I've got unmarked cars up and down my street, waiting for you to show up."

"I know. I couldn't reach you on your cell phone, so I drove by."

"My kid broke the damn phone. I had to get a new one. New number."

"What have you heard about the missing juror in the Simon case?"

"I heard you abducted her and you've been hiding from the police. Pruitt's bringing you up on charges of disobeying a superior officer and going AWOL."

Brand rubbed his temple. "Yeah, no doubt. What do you think about Pruitt?"

"You know what I think. He horned in and took over our operation, right when we were close to breaking into Castellano's inner circle. I think he's a jerk."

"But is he honest? Would he sell out?"

"He's FBI and he's a control freak. I don't think he'd do anything to jeopardize his career." Morrison paused. "Why? What's the problem?"

"Something's not right about this whole thing. He promised to pick up me and Foshee, and said he'd protect Lily Raines. He didn't do any of that. He left us swinging in the wind."

"Yeah. He said he couldn't afford to take the chance of tipping off Castellano. Apparently there's some big breakthrough in the works at one of his shipyards."

"So he sacrificed an innocent woman and a police officer for the sake of the operation?"

"He had to make a choice."

"That's total BS, Morrison. It would be okay if it were just me. But Lily Raines is completely innocent. If I hadn't stopped him, Foshee would have killed her."

"Why don't you come in? We can protect her, and maybe you won't lose your career."

"I can't and you know it. There's more. I don't think

Castellano chose me for that assignment based on my excellent track record. He'd never even looked me in the eye before the day he gave me the assignment. To him I was nothing but a bouncer."

Brand stopped. His heart pounded. He was about to tell his former boss the real reason he couldn't bring Lily in.

"Somebody set me up. I think Castellano knew I was a cop. He knew I wouldn't kill Lily. Foshee was there to be sure my prints were on the knife. He was going to make sure Lily was dead and take me back to Castellano to force me to give up the other undercover officers. When I foiled his plan, he sent thugs to my apartment. I never told anyone where I lived."

"That's quite a theory, Brand. Don't underestimate Castellano. He's a powerful man. He'd have no trouble finding out your address."

Brand frowned. "What's going on, Morrison? Since when don't you believe me?"

"I believe you, Brand. Why don't you come on in and I'll help you get this sorted out?"

"Not until I'm sure Lily's safe." He glanced at his watch. "Right now I don't know who to trust. Got to go, Lieu, before someone has a chance to trace this call."

"Brand, wait. I was going to call you. I need to meet with you. I've got some information you can use."

"What is it? Tell me now."

"I can't."

"Then I'll call you back. What's your new cell number?"

Morrison gave it to him. "Brand. I can get your girl to a safe place. Just let me know where you are."

"Sorry, Lieu. I'll call you back about a place to meet. You convince me you can keep Lily safe and I'll gladly turn her over to you. The longer she's with me, the more dangerous it gets for her."

"I'm glad you realize that."

"I realize a lot of things."

"Brand, let me pick you two up. I'll see that you get to tell your side of the story."

"Nope. I'll be in touch." He disconnected with a heavy sigh. Why the hell couldn't Morrison tell him his information over the phone? Had Pruitt gotten to him? They must have put a monitor on his phone, or Pruitt had threatened him with losing his job if he helped Brand.

Damn. He slipped back into the studio and locked the dead bolt, then pocketed the key. Was he being paranoid? Was he reading too much into what could be a series of random events?

He glanced at Lily. Her lips were slightly parted and her breaths were even and soothing in the darkness.

In Castellano's world, killing Lily would be a trial by fire—proof that a prospective member of his elite team could be trusted. Maybe it hadn't been a setup to expose Brand as a ringer.

Morrison was right about one thing though. Even though Brand's apartment wasn't in his real name, even though he took a different route home every day and kept an eye out for suspicious vehicles, Castellano probably had connections in enough places that he wouldn't have any trouble finding out where Brand lived.

But what if one of those connections was a dirty cop?

Brand couldn't take that chance. Until he could be certain Lily was beyond Castellano's reach, he couldn't let her out of his sight.

He had no one to trust to keep her safe, except himself.

Chapter Eight

Lily opened her eyes. Where was she? The room was dark, except for a sliver of light slanting across the hardwood floor. A resinous smell filled her nostrils as she blinked and sat up.

She was stiff and sore, and she'd fallen asleep in her clothes.

A disturbance of shadows near the window startled her. She tensed and grabbed a pillow. Her brain screamed *danger* as her mind conjured visions of the Cajun's terrifying smile.

Then she remembered.

It was Brand. She was with Brand. And the smells were oil paint and turpentine.

He sat up straight and looked over at her, rubbing his face with both hands. "Sorry," he said, his voice hoarse with exhaustion. "I didn't mean to wake you."

"You didn't. I dreamed someone had a knife to my throat. I dreamed they killed my father and—" She stopped as the rest of her dream came rushing into her consciousness.

"And I dreamed they killed you." Her voice broke. She shrank back against the wall and hugged the pillow.

The worst part of her dream was that it was no more of a nightmare than the reality she was living.

"I can't stand this any longer," she said in a small voice. Her stomach churned with nauseating fear. Her head swam with exhaustion. Her hands were shaking and to her utter shame, she started crying.

"Damn it," she sobbed, swiping angrily at the tears. "I need to be doing something. I need to see my father, be sure he's safe. Instead I'm stuck here with a total stranger, waiting for something to happen and I don't even know what. I can't do anything to protect him."

Brand stood and walked toward her.

She watched him approach, not knowing if the flutter of her heart was because she was glad to have him close, or because she was afraid of what he might do. Her feelings were in turmoil.

The pale light filtering through the blinds sent shadows and highlights along his neck, shoulders and lean waist. He looked strong, competent.

He sat beside her on the daybed.

She didn't move. She wasn't sure she could.

"I know you're scared," he said. "You never should have been involved in this. Don't worry, first thing in the morning, we'll check on your father. I feel sure the police have moved him to a secure facility. Now you need to sleep. You're going to need all your strength in the next couple of days."

Without thinking about the consequences, Lily scooted

closer to his comforting yet disturbing presence. She needed to touch him, to draw on his strength to help bolster her own.

It didn't make any sense that she trusted this man who'd taken her hostage, but she did. That thought triggered another—something she'd read about kidnap victims and their captors. *Stockholm syndrome.* Was she nothing more than a pathetic kidnap victim who'd come to see her captor as her protector—the only one who could keep her safe?

God, she hoped she wasn't that gullible.

To her surprise, Brand lifted his arm and draped it around her shoulders. She stiffened automatically.

"Just relax. Go to sleep."

His soft, gravelly voice rumbled through her, feeding a flame deep inside her heart—a flame that had been growing ever since he'd saved her from the Cajun's lethal knife.

She leaned her head against the hollow of his shoulder and closed her eyes, but suddenly she wasn't sleepy at all. She was wide-awake and hyperaware of his hard, warm body pressed against hers.

"Promise me you're one of the good guys," she said softly.

He went totally still.

Lily waited, not breathing. A tremor of apprehension slid through her.

Finally, to her relief, he spoke, but his words were not comforting.

"I can't promise you that. I don't feel like a good guy. I feel like a heel, allowing you to get so deeply involved. I should have been able to do something to help you."

"You saved my life." Tentatively, she put a hand on his

flat abdomen and felt the muscles quiver at her touch, felt him sigh in frustration.

"For now. There's going to be more danger. And there's nothing I can do to avoid it."

"I know. Because you don't know who to trust."

He nodded. "If I choose the wrong person, you could be facing a gun."

Lily raised her head and looked into his intense blue eyes. "But I can trust you, right?"

"Yes, you can trust me." He touched her cheek and ran his thumb lightly across her lower lip. "I *can* promise you that I'll protect you with my life."

She bent her head and grasped his forearm, wanting to hold on to the feelings he stirred inside her. Her fingers encountered laddered marks—scratches.

She sat up. "What happened to your arm?" She slid her fingertips lightly across the angry red stripes. "That was me. I scratched you."

"It's nothing. You were fighting for your life." His thumb caressed her lower lip.

Lily swallowed and let her gaze dip to his mouth. It wasn't grim or compressed now. It was relaxed. The furrow between his brows had smoothed out. He seemed more at ease than he had been the whole day.

The amazing thing was, so was she.

A deep, visceral thrill shimmered through her as he cradled the side of her face in his palm. She gasped quietly, pressing her cheek against his warm, hard fingers, never taking her eyes off him.

He searched her gaze, his blue eyes soft, questioning.

Then he dipped his head and touched his lips to hers. It might have been nothing more than a breath, but Lily felt it all the way down to her deepest core.

She tightened her thighs, trying to relieve the unslaked desire that suddenly sang through her. She lifted her head and offered her mouth to him.

His lips moved over hers, kissing her softly, tenderly. It was the sweetest kiss she'd ever experienced. And it wasn't nearly enough.

She bunched her fist in his T-shirt and pulled him closer, seeking more, craving the taste of him, the feel of his hard body pressed against hers. She strained upward, reaching for his mouth.

He pulled back, studying her intently. "Don't do this, Lily," he muttered. "You don't know what you're doing."

"Yes, I do," she lied. She had no idea what she was doing. Seeking a promise of safety from this stranger? No, she was holding fast to the only person who'd ever risked his life for hers. She needed proof of life in this dark, surreal world in which she found herself.

Whatever the reason, she was certain that if she could brand him with her body, he couldn't possibly betray her. She shuddered with erotic yearning. She ached to feel his strength surrounding her, filling her, chasing away the dark.

Wrapping her hand around his neck, she sought his mouth again.

"You don't know me." His breath whispered across her lips, stirring her more. But his words stopped her.

He was right. She didn't. But did it matter right now? When all she wanted was to feel?

"I don't need to know you," she said, even as her brain taunted her with all the things she wished she could ask him.

But there was one thing she had to know before she could go any further. The one thing that would tell her if she really could trust him.

She took a deep breath, trying to calm her racing heart. Then she looked up into his clear blue eyes. "Are you married?" *Are you a lying, cheating ass like my ex-husband?*

His brows lifted in surprise for an instant. He shook his head solemnly. "No. Not even dating."

He was telling the truth. They were too close for her to miss even the slightest flicker of hesitation.

"Me, neither," she whispered.

With a low moan, Brand pulled her to him and covered her mouth with his. He slid his fingers through her hair as he kissed her deeply, fiercely.

He lifted his head. "Be sure, Lily. Because it's been too long," he rasped, his breath hot against her mouth. "I might not be able to stop."

"I'm not asking you to stop."

An unsteady breath escaped his lips as he cradled her head and kissed her with searing promise.

She turned to him, offering herself, craving his touch.

He took her mouth totally, probing rhythmically with his tongue in an erotic imitation of lovemaking.

Overcome by desire, helpless under his sensual assault, Lily went boneless.

He leaned forward, cradling the back of her head. She let him lay her down on the daybed. He pressed his palm to her flat belly as his mouth trailed soft kisses across her cheeks and down her jaw to her neck.

"I'm so sorry I hurt you," he whispered as his lips grazed the knife cut marring her creamy skin. He gently kissed each millimeter of the wound.

"It wasn't your fault," she whispered. "I know that now."

He sought her mouth again as he slid his hand up her thigh, pushing her skirt up.

A deep sexual hunger engulfed her as he moved closer and closer to the apex of her thighs. Then she felt a featherlight touch. He slid his fingers across the crotch of her panties. Her back arched and her breath caught as his teasing strokes stirred her to a sensual frenzy she'd never before experienced.

He caressed her lightly, persistently, through the thin silk, until liquid pooled deep within her and moisture gathered. She squirmed with embarrassment and need.

He went still. "Do you want to stop? Tell me, before—"

He uttered a strangled moan as she reached for the buttons on his jeans.

He brushed her hand aside and quickly undid them himself. He sat up to peel them down his legs and off. Cool air fanned across her heated skin. She shivered.

His arousal sprang free, throbbing and pulsing against her thigh as he turned his whole attention back to her. His fingers slid beneath the damp silk of her panties and for the first time, he touched her with no barrier between his questing fingers and her most intimate flesh. Lily cried out in shock and pleasure. Then she touched him. His thick, velvety hardness pulsed against her palm. His quiet moan and sharp intake of breath told her how turned on he was. He was hovering as close to the edge as she was.

He slid his hand up her belly to her waist and unbuttoned her blouse. The lace of the bra she wore enhanced rather than inhibited the exquisite pleasure that engulfed her as he took her nipple in his mouth and gently suckled and tongued it through the thin material.

She arched toward his mouth, caught up in sensation. She'd always been shy, and sex with her ex-husband had never been completely satisfying. But suddenly she wanted to do things she'd never done before.

Her fingers closed around him boldly. She caressed him, driving him to even greater hardness.

His breath sawed in and out as he undid the clasp on the front of her bra and drew her bare nipple into his mouth. He grazed the sensitized tip with his teeth, then soothed it with his tongue.

When she thought she couldn't stand another second of his exhilarating torture, he sat up and pulled her across his lap.

Apprehension and shyness threatened to quash her desire. "I don't know how—"

"Shh. Let me do the work."

He wrapped his fingers around her waist and lifted her. She opened her legs as he held her poised above him. To her surprise, her inhibitions and awkwardness fled as she gave herself to him.

He held her poised above him, the muscles of his arms and chest bulging, as his gaze roamed over her breasts, her belly, her spread thighs, and he whispered, "Beautiful."

Her senses thrilled. Nobody had ever called her beautiful before.

She grabbed his forearms, readying herself.

He slowly lowered her onto him. When he penetrated her damp flesh, she threw her head back and nearly screamed with pleasure.

His eyes were soft and dark, like the deep blue depths of the ocean. His neck corded with strain and his cheeks turned pink as he arched upward, pressing deeper, filling her, each thrust pushing her closer to fulfillment.

Her body welcomed him. He lifted her, then lowered, then lifted her again until Lily was poised on the very edge of climax. Then he leaned forward and nuzzled her breasts, teasing first one then the other.

Her body spiraled out of control and she gasped. "Brand, please. I can't stand it."

"Come on, Lily," he growled. "Just a little more." He thrust deeply, sinking himself to the hilt inside her.

That was all it took.

Stars burst in front of Lily's eyes as she reached the pinnacle of sensation. Brand groaned and bucked, thrusting into her again and again as her climax shook him. She surrendered herself to the waves of sensation rocking her.

"That's right, Lily. Give in. Feel it," Brand whispered raggedly.

Finally, as Lily's spasms faded into tiny aftershocks, he collapsed. His quivering arms lowered her on top of him.

Lily lay against his chest, her sensitive nipples puckering at the rough, sensuous feel of his chest hair. She buried her nose in his neck and breathed deeply of the scent that was uniquely his.

He fanned his fingertips lightly over the bumps of her spine as he planted kisses on her ear, her forehead, her eyelids.

Then he turned his head and sought her mouth. His kiss was gentle, featherlike, sweet.

Lily sighed as his hand cradled her head. His body thrummed with power as his arousal slowly softened.

She felt safe. Safe and loved.

BRAND OPENED HIS EYES. Dawn had broken and the pale early morning sun crept in around the closed blinds.

He looked at Lily, asleep beside him. Her hair spread across the pillow in waves, her lips were slightly parted as she breathed softly and rhythmically. He lay still for a long time, watching her sleep. She was so lovely she made his heart ache and his eyes sting.

It astounded him that he'd actually let down his guard enough to make love to her. Equally stunning was the fact that she'd allowed him to touch her, was even eager for him.

A spear of desire shot through him at the memory of her beautiful, slender body on top of him, open to him as he let her set the pace of their joining. Watching her face as his thrusts brought her to the pinnacle of pleasure had fed his desire, until he hadn't been able to restrain himself.

He pushed a strand of dark hair back from Lily's face, his fingers trailing tenderly along her cheek.

He'd taken an even greater risk. Although his body hardened from merely touching her, he knew Lily wasn't just a casual one-nighter, nor was this merely a coming together of two strangers trying to forget for a moment that their lives were in jeopardy.

Ever since he'd first seen her, he'd recognized the threat she posed to his heart. If he wasn't careful, he could fall for her.

The thought pierced his soul with fear. That couldn't happen. He had to stay focused. His goal was to keep her alive. Emotions couldn't enter into it.

Lying there, holding her in his arms, he vowed not to go near her again. Still, even as he told himself to get up, get dressed and forget this ever happened, he knew that tearing himself away from her supple warmth, from her innocent trust, was going to be the hardest thing he'd ever done.

He didn't move. He endured the torture of her soft, naked body pressed against his. He shivered at the remembered feel of sinking into her.

His hand hovered over her pink cheek. He ached to touch her. But he took a deep breath and slowly closed his fist. He had no right.

He'd broken one of the cardinal rules of law enforcement. Never get involved with anyone connected to a case.

Of all the things he'd done that went against his oath and his training, this was the worst. He shook his head in disbelief.

What had happened to him? He'd always prided himself on his logical approach and his restraint.

A wave of self-loathing burned through him. Right now, he didn't like himself very much. He'd taken advantage of a frightened, vulnerable crime victim. He'd betrayed Lily's trust—sweet, brave Lily.

He'd tried so hard not to lie to her, but hiding the whole truth from her was also a lie. It didn't matter at this moment that he'd done it for her sake. He'd lied. And when she found out who he really was, she'd hate him.

Although he'd told her the truth about one thing. He'd never really contemplated the question she'd asked. *Was he one of the good guys?*

Had he become a cop because he'd wanted to take the unhappy world he'd grown up in and turn it on its ear? Make it happy? Make it safe? Or had he done it because it was the furthest he could get from his old man?

On the other hand, maybe Ryan had it right. Maybe he'd really become a cop to wreak vengeance on the person responsible for Patrick's death—Giovanni Castellano. God knew he'd wanted to, ever since he was thirteen and had found his brother's body.

Lily's question echoed in his ears. He'd like to think he was one of the good guys, but deep down, he knew he wasn't. He'd betrayed her trust, and when she woke up she'd realize that.

He'd promised to protect her—to keep her safe from the people who were trying to harm her. But instead he'd taken advantage of her fear and vulnerability. He'd used her to satiate his own needs.

Lily murmured his name in her sleep.

Berating himself for a weak, lonely idiot, he slid off the daybed and pulled on his clothes. He stepped over to the window.

He pushed the slats aside. It was dawn, that quiet in-between time when the world existed in muted tones of gray and blue. In the east he saw a faint pink glow.

He had to meet with Morrison, to see what information he had for him. He should have agreed to meet him last night, but Brand was much more comfortable in the light of day. That way he could watch his back.

A car pulling into the gas station across the street put his senses on full alert. The station was closed. What was that car doing?

He glanced over his shoulder at Lily, then at the door, gauging how fast he could get them out of the room.

When he peeked out the window again, the driver had gotten out and retrieved a stack of papers from his trunk. He hefted them over to a newspaper stand.

The guy was delivering today's paper. Brand's pulse quickened as he breathed a sigh of relief. He waited impatiently for the car to pull away. He needed to get a paper so he could find out what the media had to say about the missing juror number seven.

Keeping an eye on Lily to be sure she was still asleep, he shrugged into his long-sleeved shirt, tucked his weapon into his waistband and unlocked the double dead bolt on the studio door.

After easing it shut, he locked it behind him, then bounded down the stairs and across the street. He'd seen vending machines near the newspaper stand. At the thought of food—even stale vending machine food—his stomach rumbled. Damn, he hoped they weren't empty.

He bought a couple of sodas, some cheese-flavored crackers and a paper.

He looked around cautiously, but the colorless dawn didn't expose any lurking figures. The street was deserted.

Quickly, he crossed to the office building and hurried back upstairs.

He unlocked the door, slipped inside and relocked it. When he looked up, the daybed was empty. Alarm sent his pulse pounding.

Then he realized that the bathroom door was closed. Relief burned through him. Rationality told him nothing could have happened to her in the few minutes he'd been gone, but his reaction wasn't logical, it was emotional.

The door opened and Lily came out, finger-combing her hair. She smiled. "Good morning."

"Morning. Sorry if I woke you," he said. "I got us some food and a newspaper."

"Great, thanks. I'm starving."

He couldn't take his eyes off her pink cheeks. His stubble had rubbed her skin. He ran his hand along his jaw. "While you eat I'll clean up." Setting down the newspaper and the snacks, he headed into the bathroom.

As the door closed, Lily sat on the edge of the daybed and ripped open a package of cheese crackers. She wolfed them down with one of the sodas. She left the rest for Brand. Her hunger assuaged, she lay back and closed her eyes.

A thrill of desire arrowed through her as she recalled Brand's strong body enveloping hers, and the exquisite feel of him sinking into her.

She heard the water running in the bathroom. Opening her eyes, she sat up. It was the first time she'd had even a few minutes alone. She ought to make the most of them.

She glanced toward the door to the hall, but the double dead bolt was locked, and Brand had the key in his pocket.

She didn't know what she'd do if she escaped, anyway. She had to admit she was safer with Brand than on her own.

So she surveyed the tiny studio and her gaze lit on the canvases stacked against the wall. He hadn't wanted her to go through them. He'd said he wanted her away from the window, but what if he'd had another reason not to want her snooping around?

Glancing at the closed bathroom door, she rose from the bed. There were a dozen or more canvases turned face to the wall. She flipped one around, then another and another. Then she saw it. The painting he hadn't wanted her to find.

BRAND RUBBED HIS newly shaven cheeks. He'd found a package of disposable razors under the sink. He'd had to use flower-scented soap to shave and wash up, but he felt much better.

When he exited the bathroom, Lily was sitting on the stool in front of Cassie's easel.

"Did you eat?" he asked.

She didn't answer.

"Lily?"

She sat as still as a statue, her face a pale orb, her eyes wide and filled with hurt.

"Lily," he said again. "What's the matter?"

She was staring at something. He turned to look at whatever held her attention.

What he saw nearly stopped his heart.

She was looking at an unframed oil painting propped against the wall.

He'd forgotten that Cassie had painted him in his police

academy dress uniform. He'd liked the painting, but she'd wanted to work on it some more. She wasn't satisfied with the look in his eye. His expression was too serious, too stiff, she'd said.

He faced Lily, a hollow regret sinking deep into his chest. She'd hate him now. Worse than that, she'd never trust him again.

And if she didn't trust him, he couldn't keep her safe.

Lily had heard Brand's questions, but she couldn't answer him. She couldn't take her eyes off the portrait.

Her senses had gone numb. Her perception of reality had faded into yet another nightmare, and her father's voice rang in her ears.

Nobody's more dangerous than a rogue cop.

Slowly, her brain began to make sense out of what she was seeing.

She knew the stiff, proud figure in the painting was Brand. In a police uniform. The artist had caught his intensity and dogged determination in the expression on his face. It was a wonderful portrait.

Lily's fingers and toes tingled like waking limbs. Her heart had lodged itself somewhere in the back of her throat, and suddenly she realized she was angrier and more frightened than she'd ever been in her life.

Not even Foshee's terrifying threats nor the gun held to her head in the restaurant had sent cutting shards of panic through her the way discovering this painting had. Her body quaked with fury. Her heart broke with betrayal.

"Lily, let me explain—"

She quelled him with a glance. The face in the painting

was younger, less lined than the one looking at her in faint horror now. In the painting, Brand's cheeks still held the blush of youthful pride he must have felt the day he graduated from the police academy.

The academy. The man standing before her—the man to whom she'd given herself in the night—was a cop. *A cop gone bad.*

What else could explain his refusal to take her to the police? Still, he'd saved her from Castellano. He'd helped the Cajun follow and threaten her, but he'd held her and made love to her and kept her safe. Her brain whirled with conflicting thoughts and emotions.

"Lily—"

"Don't talk to me," she said coldly. "Unlock the door. I'm getting out of here." She'd already straightened her clothes and slipped on her shoes.

"No. You can't. We don't know who might be out there, waiting."

"Oh. Do you think whoever is out there will be worse than who's standing here in front of me, lying to me?" She crossed her arms and lifted her chin. "How can I believe anything you say? You're a police officer. And yet you let me be set up to be killed. Worse—you left my father vulnerable. How could you do that to a fellow police officer?"

"There's a lot you don't know. You have to trust me."

"I can never trust you." Her face grew warm as she thought about how safe and right she'd felt in his arms. Apparently his body could lie as easily as his mouth. "You lied to me."

"No, I didn't."

"Well, I don't know how you define lying, but you sure

as hell didn't tell me the truth. I don't feel like arguing over semantics, if you don't mind. Now are you going to let me out of here or not?"

"No, I'm not. You've got to listen to me." He reached for her but she recoiled, her hands up in a don't-you-dare-touch-me gesture.

"I will not listen to any more of your lies."

He backed off and stood there, his hands out. "I'll tell you what I can. I've been undercover for three years, working to bring down Castellano. I couldn't blow the operation by refusing to do the job Castellano himself assigned to me. There are other lives at stake. Two other undercover officers."

He spread his hands in supplication. "From the moment I saw you—" He stopped and took a deep breath. "I had to go along, or I'd be placing your life and the lives of others in danger. If Castellano suspected I was a cop, Springer and Carson's lives would be over."

"The other undercover officers? What about them? Are they on the run, too?"

He shook his head. "As far as I know, they're still working on the docks. I'm the one who got the assignment. I'm the one who was set up to kill you. Once everything went sour, I had no choice but to grab you and run. I didn't know who to trust. I still don't."

Lily took a step toward him. "Well, since you're being so *honest,* explain that to me. You're a cop. How can you not trust your fellow officers?"

"My contact, the FBI agent in charge of the task force, hung me out to dry. He promised he'd have Foshee and me picked up before we left the courtroom. Nobody showed up, so I had to go with Foshee to your apartment. He was determined to kill you. I had to improvise."

Lily's head swam. He was a cop, yet he was running from both Castellano and the police. He'd lied to her. And he'd denied being a police officer—hadn't he?

She glanced at the daybed and a splinter of remembered desire lodged painfully in her heart. What a fool she'd been. She'd believed in him.

I had to improvise.

Hurt arrowed through her middle. It felt like heartache, like betrayal. "I suppose you were improvising last night, too?"

A shadow of pain crossed his face and he opened his mouth. "Lily, I'm sorry. I never should have—"

"Don't." She held up a hand. "Don't bother lying to me any more. Just move out of the way and let me leave."

In utter desperation she pushed past him. He caught her upper arms.

"You're not going anywhere. Not until I can be sure you're safe." His blue eyes were intense.

She shrugged free. "Don't touch me. The farther I can get from you, the safer I'll be." She rattled the doorknob. "Unlock the damn door!"

"Lily. Stop. You need to calm down."

"Calm down? Are you kidding me?" She stared at him wide-eyed. "You're holding me hostage. For all I know you betrayed your fellow officers like you betrayed my father and me. If you don't let me go, I'll start screaming."

Brand turned her to face him. "You try that and I'll be forced to gag and bind you. Understand?"

She winced at the look on his face. How had she ever thought his blue eyes were kind? Right now they were as opaque and hard as lapis lazuli.

His fingers squeezed her arm. "Do you?" he snapped.

She tried to kick him, but he dodged her and pulled her up tightly against him, holding her so she couldn't move.

She felt the hardness of his body against hers, and an echo of the safety and comfort that he exuded washed over her senses. She shook her head violently. They weren't true—these signals her body received from his. He wasn't safe. Not in any sense of the word.

Brand's hand cradled the back of her head while his other arm held her tight. His breath was hot against her ear. "Do you understand?"

"Yes," she said through gritted teeth. "I understand."

"Are you going to be quiet and still?"

She nodded, trying not to breathe in his evocative male scent. She would never again be able to smell Ivory soap or mint mouthwash without thinking of him. He'd branded her body and soul with his fierce, passionate lovemaking, and now she could barely distinguish danger from safety.

She had to guard against him now more than ever, because he'd slipped beneath her defenses. She hadn't known she was so vulnerable.

"I'm going to arrange to see my lieutenant today. If he's willing to help us, I can probably get you into a safe house before the end of the day."

She frowned. "Really?" She heard the hope in her voice, felt it flutter in her chest. Maybe once she was under the protection of the police, she could see her father. And maybe, once she was away from Brand, she could get rid of the potent attraction she felt for him. She wrenched away from his grip.

"Well, that's good, Brand, or whoever you really are, because I'm not staying around you one minute longer than I have to. Now leave me alone."

Chapter Nine

Brand told the taxi driver to stop in front of the Island Bay Hotel and Casino. He'd arranged this meeting with Morrison only fifteen minutes ago, so that his lieutenant would have to rush to make it.

"I won't wait, Lieu," Brand had warned him. "If you're not there, I'm leaving."

Morrison had sworn he'd be there—alone.

Brand couldn't figure out what Morrison had for him that he couldn't say over the phone. He didn't like the way Morrison was acting. Not one bit. It felt wrong, just like the whole operation.

Before yesterday, he'd have sworn Morrison was the last person on the planet who'd betray him. But today he didn't trust him. He couldn't afford to trust anyone.

He got out of the car with Lily at his side and paid the fare, careful to keep his face averted from the driver. He knew from his experience as a detective that all the cabs in the area had been given his and Lily's descriptions. He could only hope this cabbie was as unconcerned about the two of them as he appeared to be.

As he rounded the back of the car and stepped onto the sidewalk, Lily's eyes snapped with suspicion.

"I thought you told your lieutenant to meet us at the Biloxi Belle."

Brand nodded and grabbed her hand. "The Belle's parking garage backs up to this one. Come on. I don't want to be recognized. We'll cut through."

He'd debated leaving her locked inside the studio. But the idea of letting her out of his sight for any length of time was as abhorrent as the thought of leaving her alone and defenseless, trapped in a locked room.

He wasn't planning to be gone more than a half hour, but still, anything could happen.

It wasn't beyond the realm of possibility that either Castellano or the police would search for family in their efforts to find him. It wouldn't be a huge leap to connect a studio rented in the name of Cassandra Gallagher to Brand Gallagher.

If his cover was blown with Castellano, he had no doubt the crime boss knew his real name.

Brand led Lily through the opulent lobby of the Island Bay Hotel and Casino, until they got to the elevators. He punched the button labeled Parking.

"You aren't going to do it, are you?"

Brand watched the numbers light up on the elevator sign. "Do what?"

"Turn me over to your lieutenant."

"I'm going to see what he has to say."

"I thought you trusted him."

"I did, once. Now I'm not so sure."

"Why?"

The bell rang and the elevator doors opened. He wrapped his arm around her, feeling her instantly go rigid. He pulled her inside with him. An older woman with a plastic cup full of quarters looked at the button he punched.

"So you two have been here all night, too? Did you have good luck?" she asked. "I did."

Lily started to speak, but Brand squeezed her hand and cut his eyes at her. She clamped her mouth shut, fury radiating from her like heat.

Brand smiled at the woman. "We did all right."

The elevator bell rang. As the doors slid open, the cacophony caused by the people and the machines on the casino floor swelled to deafening proportions.

The woman stepped off the elevator, turned and said something, but the clang of winning bells, the din of coins crashing into metal trays and the sound effects coming from hundreds of flashing, brightly lit slot machines drowned out her words.

Brand smiled and nodded as the doors slid shut.

Lily jerked her hand away from his and shook it. "Ouch! What did you think I was going to do? Beg her to save me? Steal her quarters and run?" She stuck her chin out and frowned up at him.

"Listen to me. We can't afford to draw any attention to ourselves. Law enforcement all along the Coast have orders to watch for us."

She started to speak, but he raised his hand to stop her. "We're fugitives. Our descriptions are everywhere. Today's paper carried a small feature about the missing juror. They didn't identify you, except to name you as Juror Number Seven, but they did have a picture, probably taken after the verdict. You're standing by your car."

"So why isn't that reason enough to turn ourselves over to the police and ask for their protection?"

Brand ignored her biting comment. An ominous thought had occurred to him. "Look at you. You're still in the outfit you wore in court. You look exactly like that picture." The blouse was wrinkled, but she still looked like she'd be comfortable walking on a fashion runway.

She certainly didn't look like she belonged with him in his worn jeans, once-white T-shirt and wrinkled, unbuttoned dress shirt. But his attire didn't matter.

"We've got to get you some new clothes."

"What about you?"

He glanced at the mirror that covered one wall of the elevator. "I look pretty damned generic."

"Not really."

What did she mean by that? He frowned at their reflections. Did they look like gamblers that had been up all night, or desperate fugitives on the run? He couldn't decide.

The bell rang and the light on the parking level button went out.

"Let's go," he said, sliding his arm around Lily's waist.

She stiffened. "Where are we meeting him?"

"On Parking Level Four, near the elevators."

He led her through the glass-enclosed parking lobby and into the concrete parking garage.

"The elevators are over there," Lily pointed out.

"We're taking the stairs," Brand snapped. "Now be

quiet. If there's anyone on the stairs I want to know before we run into them."

He pushed open the door marked Fire Stairs and started climbing. He kept hold of Lily's hand, making sure she stayed close behind him. He moved his weapon to the front of his jeans and rested his right hand on it.

They went up, past the doors marked Two and Three. He paused at the door that read Four. Through the tiny pane of wire-reinforced glass, he surveyed the area. He could see the elevators across the way, but he didn't see the lieutenant anywhere.

Damn. He'd warned him that he wouldn't wait. Still, he had to check the area. Morrison was a careful guy. Maybe he was staying out of sight until he was sure Brand hadn't been followed.

Easing open the level four door, Brand took in the space around him with one swift glance. He didn't see anyone. He'd known the parking garage would be shadowy, but as he'd hoped, the top level was essentially empty. There were only a couple of cars.

He didn't recognize either one, but that didn't mean anything. Morrison could have brought his wife's car, or even borrowed one from police impound.

Behind him Lily tugged against his tight grip. He let go of her hand and pulled his weapon.

Looking her in the eye, he mouthed, "Stay with me. Walk where I walk, and if you hear anything, duck. This is life or death. Understand?"

Her face turned pale and her gaze flickered from one part of the garage to another then back to him. She nodded.

Brand didn't know if she would obey him or not. But her brown eyes were clear, and when he moved she obediently followed right in his footsteps. Maybe she trusted him enough to believe that she was safest with him.

He could only hope.

He edged along the wall with Lily right behind him. He paused, listening. He had to step into the open in order to examine the two cars.

Just as he moved away from the relative safety of the solid wall, the elevator bell rang.

Someone was coming.

As the heavy doors creaked open, Brand wrapped his left arm around Lily's waist, both to protect her and to use her body to hide the gun in his hand.

Lily's breath caught.

"Shh," he hissed in her ear. "Pretend we snuck up here for a quick grope."

Her body trembled, but she gamely wrapped her arms around his neck and pressed her cheek to his. "Don't get any ideas. I still don't trust you."

"You've made that abundantly clear," he whispered back, watching out of the corner of his eye as a couple exited the elevator. The young woman stopped short when she saw them, but her companion urged her on.

"Come on. Don't worry about them. They're not thinking about mugging anybody," Brand heard the man mutter.

Lily clung to Brand's neck, tortured by his closeness and struck by the absurdity of their situation. His muscled arm around her waist held her protectively and provocatively molded against his body, yet in his other hand he clutched a deadly weapon.

They were sneaking around the casino's parking garage as if they were crooks, but one quick glance had convinced the couple that she and Brand weren't dangerous.

Brand was alert and jittery, expecting an ambush at every corner, an enemy in every shadow. He was so paranoid, so certain that one of his fellows was a traitor. It was absurd that she felt so safe in his arms.

He was a mass of contradiction and she was a mass of frayed nerves.

She stood on tiptoes and watched over his shoulder as the man and woman walked toward their car.

"Where's your lieutenant?" she whispered in his ear.

He drew in a quick breath. "He'll be here."

Lily heard the doubt in his voice. He was afraid he'd been betrayed again. Despite her apprehension, her heart went out to him.

"What are the man and woman doing?"

"They're just about to reach the first car."

Brand's hand holding the gun pressed into her side. He kissed her cheek. His fingers spread over the small of her back. "Good. They'll be gone soon. Morrison's probably waiting for them to leave."

Just as he spoke, the woman grabbed her companion's arm and screamed.

Brand whirled and in one motion, pushed Lily behind him and pointed his weapon.

The woman screamed again. The man grabbed her. "Oh, my God!" he gasped.

Brand moved toward them, his gun still at the ready. "Hold it!" he shouted. "I'm a police officer."

Lily followed him. As they approached the dark sedan, she caught a glimpse of what had made the woman scream. A man lay beside the car with blood pooling on the concrete beneath his shoulders.

Lily's stomach turned over. She covered her mouth. "Oh, dear God, no!"

Brand gestured toward the couple with the barrel of his weapon. "Move away from the vehicle," he said. "Do it now! Is this your car?"

The man put out his hand to shield his wife. "No. Ours is th-that one." He pointed to a light blue car several parking spaces away.

The woman whimpered and clutched at his sleeve. "Don't hurt us, please. We have children."

"Get out of here!" Brand lowered his gun.

Lily felt the tension radiating from him. The barrel of his gun was unsteady. He never stopped looking around, never left his back unguarded.

"What? Why?" the man said. "What about the man? We should call someone—"

"Get in your car and get out of here. After you exit the parking garage, call 911."

The man hesitated, glancing toward the body.

"Go!"

The two turned and ran up the hill to their car. After a few seconds its engine roared to life and they sped away with a screech of tires.

Brand bent over the man. "Morrison! Gary!" His voice cracked. He felt the man's neck for a pulse.

Lily held her breath.

"He's alive."

"What—what happened to him?"

Brand quickly examined him. "He has a bulletproof vest on, but he's been shot in the neck. Hang in there, Lieu. Help is coming."

"Brand," the man whispered.

"Morrison, you're going to be okay." Brand's voice shook. "What the hell happened?"

"—followed."

An ominous gurgle bubbled up from the injured man's throat. Lily's entire body went cold. This was Morrison. Brand's lieutenant. The only man he trusted.

"Who followed you? Where are they now?" Brand leaned close.

"I spotted 'em. Drew my weapon. They—didn't play by the rules." Morrison's pinched mouth turned up slightly. "Shot me above the—vest."

"We've got an ambulance on its way. You're going to be fine."

Lily heard a noise from the stairwell. "Brand, someone's coming."

Brand straightened, listening.

"Go. Get out of here," Morrison gasped.

Lily tugged on Brand's shoulder. "That couple called 911. It might be the police."

Brand hesitated.

"Brand—get her out of here. You were right." Morrison sucked in a rattling breath. "They found out—I was meeting—you. Pruitt wouldn't—"

The sound Lily had heard turned into footsteps—more than one set.

The bleat of a siren split the air.

"Pruitt wouldn't what? Lieutenant!"

Morrison coughed and blood spewed from his mouth.

Brand pulled up Morrison's pant leg and retrieved the backup service revolver from his ankle holster. He put it into his lieutenant's trembling hands and leaned close to his ear. "Police are on their way, Lieu. Shoot first. I'll cover you as long as I can."

Then he rose and grabbed Lily's waist.

"Behind the post," he said, pushing her ahead of him. He trained his gun on the fire stairs.

Lily ran for the concrete pillar.

Brand was right behind her. He stuck his head out and jerked it back. "Damn it! It's Castellano's men," he whispered. "And they're armed."

He nodded toward the ramp leading down to level three. "Run, Lily. Don't stop until you reach the street. Then call the police."

"But that couple already did—"

"Maybe, maybe not. Remember, you don't know who to trust."

Lily peered at the fire stair door, at the ramp to level three, then at Brand's lieutenant, fighting for his life on the concrete floor. "What about you? What about him?"

"We'll be all right."

She saw something shiny under the back fender of the lieutenant's car. It was a gun.

The stair door crashed open. Lily had only a split second to make a decision.

There was only one thing she could do. She couldn't leave Brand here to face the killers alone.

She dove across the open space and reached under the car. Her fingers barely closed around the lieutenant's service revolver just as two men burst through the stairway door, weapons in hand.

She crouched behind the lieutenant's car and quickly ejected the magazine. There were several rounds left. She slapped it back into place.

"Lily!" Brand shouted.

She nodded at him, earning her a glare before he turned his attention back to the men.

One guy saw her. "Hey! There she is!" He fired, barely missing her cheek.

She ducked, then braced herself to shoot.

Brand got off two shots before the other man started shooting at him.

Lily's hands shook. Her father had taught her how to shoot a 9 mm a long time ago. She knew her way around a gun. But she'd never shot at anything alive before—not even a rabbit or a squirrel.

She held her breath, aimed and squeezed the trigger. One of the men yelped and grabbed his shoulder.

Her heart jumped into her throat. She'd hit him!

Brand fired two more quick rounds, then ducked back behind the pillar.

He gestured with his head. She read his signal loud and clear.

Get over here.

She peered over the car's back, looking for the men. The

man she'd shot held his arm. The other was braced to shoot. As she watched, he fired three times at Brand. Concrete shards flew as bullets ricocheted off the pillar.

She shot at him but missed.

Brand sent her a telling look, nodded and leaned out, firing off several quick rounds.

He was giving her cover. She took a deep breath and dashed for the pillar, shooting wildly. She gritted her teeth, expecting to feel the bite of a bullet in her side at any second.

She made it without being hit. It was a miracle, with all the bullets flying.

Brand stopped her headlong flight with one hard arm, pulling her into his side. Setting her back against the pillar, he held her while he shot again, then ducked to safety as the two men launched a volley of slugs at them.

"What the hell were you thinking?" he snapped.

Lily's breath rasped through her fear-clogged throat. She held Morrison's gun in both shaking hands, its cold steel pressed between her abdomen and Brand's.

His breaths were harsh in her ear, his chest rose and fell rapidly against hers. His heart pounded.

"I saw the gun," she panted. "Figured we needed it."

He pulled his head back to look down at her. "You shoot like a pro."

"My father taught me." Lily heard more sirens. She clutched Brand's shirt. "I hear police sirens. That couple must have called 911."

He angled around the pillar, shot and pulled back. "Run up the ramp to five," he commanded. "I'll cover you."

"What about you?"

"I'll be right behind you."

The sirens got louder. She heard the screech of tires as a vehicle roared up the ramp on the level below. The hollow echo inside the parking garage distorted the sounds. What was it? An ambulance? A police car?

She took a deep breath, made herself let go of Brand's shirt and ran.

The pop-pop of gunfire followed her. She heard the zing of a ricocheting bullet after it hit the garage floor next to her foot.

She reached the ramp and darted up it as fast as she could, turning and firing a couple of times, taking care to give Brand's pillar a wide berth. When she reached the top, she hid behind the concrete guardrail and fired two more rounds, giving Brand the cover he'd given her.

He vaulted up the ramp just as an ambulance roared up beside Morrison's unmoving form.

The two gunmen took one look at the ambulance and stopped shooting. They turned tail and ducked back through the stairwell door.

"Let's go!" Brand took Lily's hand and sprinted across the open expanse of the parking lot toward a glass door at the far end. If they were lucky, it would lead to a crosswalk from the parking lot to the hotel.

"What about your lieutenant?" Lily asked.

"The paramedics will take care of him."

"But who shot him?"

Brand didn't stop to consider Lily's question. He heard the stairwell door behind them creak open and his heart slammed against his chest.

The gunmen had taken the stairs to the fifth level.

"Go!" He pushed Lily toward the doors and turned back to face their pursuers.

For the first time, he had a split second to look at their faces. He recognized them. They were two of Castellano's favorite musclemen.

The one Lily had winged held his gun awkwardly in his left hand, but his partner looked perfectly healthy and capable of killing.

"Give it up, Brand. Mr. Castellano wants to see you." The man raised his weapon. "I'd suggest you come with us. We'll send someone to pick up your girlfriend."

In answer, Brand dove behind the concrete guardrail and fired off several rounds.

The air around him exploded with gunfire as he ducked down and checked his magazine. Only six rounds left.

Damn it. He gauged the distance to the glass doors. With any luck at all, he'd make it.

He raised up and shot four times, just as a piercing wail announced the approach of a police car.

Brand sprinted across the open space and through the doors.

Lily was waiting for him inside the glass-enclosed corridor, holding a mop in her hands. As Brand watched in amazement she shoved the handle of the mop through the door latches.

She turned to him. "Maybe it'll slow them down."

"Good job." He grinned. "Learn that from your dad?"

"No. From TV."

"Hah! We've got a chance to lose them. Come on. Let's get out of here."

"What should I do with the gun?" She held it clutched tightly in her fingers. She shrugged. "No pockets."

Brand assessed her. Her hair was tangled, her eyes were huge and frightened in her pale face and her hands trembled. But as he studied her, she raised her chin and looked him straight in the eye.

He reached for her, wincing in hollow regret when she flinched.

"It's okay," he said. "Stick it in your waistband." He tugged on her blouse.

She recoiled, and pulled the tail of her blouse out of her skirt herself. Then she sucked in a deep breath and slid the pistol into place. She shivered as the cool metal touched her skin.

They walked through the glass crosswalk toward another set of double doors.

Two men pushed through. They were engrossed in an argument about a poker tournament and didn't even spare Brand or Lily a glance.

Inside, they found themselves on a mezzanine over-looking the main floor of the Biloxi Belle Casino. The din was deafening.

Brand searched the corners of the vast room, looking for a gift shop or boutique. Didn't all these fancy casino hotels have shopping facilities?

He spotted a sign in the far corner of the floor. He pointed. "We need to get over there."

Lily looked where he'd pointed. "Why? What's that?"

"I'm hoping it's a shopping court."

He put his hand in the small of her back and guided her to the escalator. He never let down his guard, not even for a second. He was taking a deadly risk, possibly endangering innocent lives. But he had to hope the police had slowed down Castellano's men.

As the escalator took them down to the casino floor, Brand checked out the exits. The closest one was on the south side. But the easiest to navigate was on the west, near their destination.

A familiar blue uniform caught his eye. A police officer had just entered the casino through the south doors and was sweeping the room with his gaze.

Brand quickly propelled Lily toward the shopping court. His number one priority was to get her safely away.

Now that someone had shot Morrison, he was even more convinced that he couldn't trust anyone—not even the police.

Chapter Ten

By the time they returned to the studio, Lily was shivering with a combination of exhaustion and reaction to the gun fight. They'd run the twenty or so blocks from the casino. It was a good thing Brand had bought her new clothes at the hotel's exclusive boutique.

The acid-washed jeans, designer T-shirt and slip-on tennis shoes were a lot easier to run in than her tight skirt and pumps, but their price tags had shocked her.

She'd been surprised when Brand pulled out a credit card, but he'd assured her the police already knew they'd been in at least one of the two casinos, because of Morrison. It wouldn't matter if a credit card charge came in. The bigger problem would be the store's record of what they'd bought. If detectives obtained that information, they'd have an updated description of what Lily was wearing.

Brand unlocked the door to the studio.

"Wait here. I want to make sure everything's okay." He entered with his gun drawn. A few seconds later he gestured for her. "All clear."

She headed straight for the bathroom. With shaky

fingers she pulled the lieutenant's gun out of her waistband and gingerly set it on the counter.

Tremors spread up her arms and through her entire body as she stared at the weapon, then at her hands.

She'd shot a man. Her eyes stung and her throat closed up. Granted she'd nearly missed him, and the wound had barely slowed him down, but that wasn't the point.

The point was she'd shot him. And with hardly any hesitation. Of course, he'd been shooting at her and Brand, so her shot was self-defense.

That didn't make her feel one bit better.

She studied her reflection in the mirror. She was white as a ghost. Her eyes were rimmed with dark circles and her lips were tight and white at the corners.

All at once her knees buckled, her stomach lurched and she dropped to the floor. She pulled herself up enough to hang her head over the toilet as heaving spasms wracked her.

By the time her stomach was empty and the spasms had finally stopped, Brand was at her side with a warm, wet cloth.

She took it gratefully and covered her face, relishing the warmth as she waited to see if her stomach was going to rebel again. After a few seconds she sat back against the door and lifted her hair to run the cloth around the back of her neck.

When she finally opened her eyes, Brand was watching her, a thoughtful expression on his face. "You okay?" he asked.

She shook her head. "I shot a man." Her mouth filled with acrid saliva. She pressed the cloth to her cheeks.

"A man who was going to kill you."

"Somehow, knowing that doesn't make me feel a whole lot better."

"I know. But you should be proud. You did a great job out there. As good as any cop—especially considering you're a rookie." He sent her a reassuring smile and dropped to the floor beside her.

She didn't feel like smiling back at him or allowing him to get any closer. She felt like crying. She was so tired. So scared and so damned confused.

She lowered the cloth. The question that had nagged at her from the moment they'd seen Morrison rose in her mind.

"Who shot your lieutenant?"

Brand frowned. She'd asked the same question when they were running from Castellano's gunmen.

"I don't know. But I doubt it was the two goons who chased us. Why would they shoot him then stick around waiting to see if we showed up?"

"They wouldn't. Unless they knew we were coming to meet him. But if that were the case, why shoot him first? Why not take out all of us at once?" As soon as Lily said the words, what little color remained in her face drained away.

Brand's heart squeezed in compassion. The danger she'd been exposed to in the last few days was foreign to her. It didn't matter that her father had been on the job for over twenty years. As much as he'd taught her, he'd obviously shielded her from the worst aspects of his work.

"There were two of them," he said. "If they'd waited, they would have been facing three of us, not two."

"Or they didn't want to take the chance that Morrison would tell you what he knew."

Brand nodded. "That makes sense. But how did they know we were meeting him? Or where we would be?"

"Someone in the police department is feeding information to Castellano."

"That's what I've thought all along." Brand nodded. "But no one knew Morrison was meeting us."

"You don't think it's him?"

"No. I've known Morrison for years. He was my lieutenant for five years and my contact for the first year I was undercover."

"But what did he have to tell you that he couldn't say over the phone?"

"I don't know. He didn't say much. Said he'd been followed. He said something about Pruitt."

"Pruitt?"

"My contact for the past two years. He's with the FBI."

Lily must have heard the suspicion in his voice, because she sent him a sidelong glance. "You don't trust him."

"Not much."

"What did Morrison say?"

He shook his head. "All I got was 'Pruitt wouldn't.'"

Lily pushed herself up, but slipped back to the floor with a moan. Brand stood and offered his hand. She took it. When she stood upright, she swayed.

"Hey," he said, putting his arm around her. "Be careful. You're exhausted and you have nothing in your stomach."

She leaned close.

He gave in to a dangerous urge and buried his nose in her hair. The faint smell of coconut stirred his desire. He pulled her closer and cradled the back of her head in his palm.

He felt a shaky sigh ripple through her. Her breath warmed the skin of his neck. He slid his fingers beneath her hair and massaged the knotted muscles in her neck and shoulders.

"Brand?" Her voice was small and hesitant, and the question in it shot straight to his loins. The foreign urge he'd been fighting from the first moment he laid eyes on her slipped beneath his careful reserve—the urge to care for her, to protect her, to love her.

As if she sensed the change in him, she pulled away, avoiding his gaze. "Do you think there's any toothpaste in here?" she asked tightly.

He reluctantly let her go. "There's mouthwash." He opened the cabinet behind the mirror and pulled out a bottle of green liquid.

"Thanks." She grabbed the bottle and clutched it in front of her like a shield.

She wanted him to leave.

He exited the bathroom and went over to the window, sucking in a deep breath to calm his racing heart. He reminded himself of his vow not to touch her. She didn't want *him*. She just wanted her life back.

If he had the power, he'd give her what she wanted. He'd planned on turning her over to Morrison. But whoever had betrayed him and the entire police force had made that impossible.

Lifting the edge of the blinds, he checked the street below. He was certain they hadn't been followed, but what if whoever was leaking information to Castellano knew about Cassie's studio?

The snitch could be anyone on the force. Before he'd

been given the undercover assignment, Brand had shared a few tidbits about his life with some of his fellow officers. If he had been a bit more reticent than most, it was because he hadn't wanted to get into the melodrama of growing up in an alcoholic household.

Still, there was no one he could eliminate. Not even the lieutenant or his fellow undercover officers. Certainly not Pruitt. Not only did he not trust the FBI agent, he had no idea what information Pruitt had been given about him.

For the first time, Brand faced the raw truth—Morrison had been his last hope. There was literally no one he could trust now.

On a visceral level he had known it, but he'd never admitted to himself that even his closest peers could be working for Castellano. It was an abhorrent thought that a cop would turn on his fellow officers, but it had happened before. And it would happen again.

If the traitor knew about his brother's wife's studio, he and Lily were sitting ducks. He had to be extra vigilant until he could figure out another place for them to hide.

His cell phone rang. It was Pruitt. For an instant, Brand considered turning off the phone, but the displayed number flashed, mocking him. He pressed the answer key.

"Are you happy now, Gallagher? You got Morrison shot."

"Did he tell you he was meeting me?"

Pruitt cursed. "Hell, no. If he had, he wouldn't be in surgery now."

Brand went cold. "How is he?"

"It's touch and go. He had on a vest, but slugs caught him in the shoulder and the neck."

"Where is he? Which hospital?"

"I'm not answering any more questions. I'm asking them," Pruitt growled. "Where are you?"

"What did Morrison have to tell me?"

"Gallagher, I'm warning you—"

"No, *I'm* warning you! If you would be up-front with me just once, I might be persuaded to trust you. But you keep lying to me."

He heard a heavy sigh on the other end of the line. "There's a leak."

Brand spat a curse. "You're just now figuring that out?" Was Pruitt baiting him with information he already knew, hoping to lure him in? "I thought it was you," he snapped.

The FBI agent snorted. "You think I'd risk jeopardizing this operation? This is a once-in-a-lifetime opportunity for me. If I can bring down Castellano, I can write my own ticket. If I knew who's leaking intel to Castellano, I'd kill him myself."

"What about Springer and Carson?"

"They're still undercover. I've been in touch with them on a daily basis. We're almost ready to blow Castellano's arms-smuggling operation right out of the water." Pruitt paused. "I think the leak is someone closer to the administration. I think Morrison knows."

"You think that's what he wanted to tell me? Who the leak is? That's interesting, because the last thing he said was your name."

"You talked to him? I thought he was unconscious."

"So, Special Agent Pruitt, if the lieutenant had vital information to give, why didn't he share it with you?"

"Because he didn't want me to get all the glory."

Wrong answer. Brand shook his head. Pruitt had just given himself away. "You don't really believe that. You're not that dumb." The FBI agent had to be running on ego. "Morrison suspects you, doesn't he? That's why he wanted to talk to me."

"You're on awfully thin ice, Gallagher."

"I've been on thin ice before. Where is he? County General?"

"You're AWOL. There's no way I'm giving you that information."

"I'll find out on my own if you won't tell me."

"You go right ahead. We'll be waiting for you."

"Yeah? Fine. You spend your time and energy waiting for me. What about Lily's dad?"

"I told you we have that covered."

"Covered? Does that mean he's been picked up and placed in protective custody?"

"We're on it. You get in here and maybe I'll answer that question for you."

Brand angrily punched the disconnect button. "Son of a—"

The bathroom door opened and Lily came out. Her face was clean and shiny, her hair was slightly damp, and she looked if not a hundred percent better, at least seventy percent. The small T-shirt with its sequined logo clung to her slim figure, outlining her enticing curves that were emphasized by the low-cut jeans. A sliver of her flat, smooth belly showed between the bottom of the T-shirt and the low-riding waistband of the jeans.

Her wide eyes sent him a message he'd give anything to avoid. That despite her I-can-take-care-of-myself attitude, she looked to him to protect her. He saw trust in her gaze, and it terrified him.

Who was he kidding? He couldn't risk her life any longer. He had to take her to the police. He was being selfish and arrogant, keeping her here with him.

She sat down on the daybed and clasped her hands.

Brand looked at her more closely. Her eyes were red. She'd been crying. His heart twisted in compassion and guilt.

"I need to check on my father," she said quietly without looking at him.

"Okay."

Her gaze snapped to his. "Okay?"

He nodded and dug his phone out of his pocket. He tossed it to her. "It's the third phone number in the queue."

He hoped like hell that Pruitt was just baiting him. Surely the task force had transported Joe Raines to a secure facility by now.

Lily grasped the cell phone like a lifeline. "You're going to let me dial it?"

He shrugged. "One of us has got to trust the other."

She raised her brows, then nodded as she searched for the number and punched the call button.

An unfamiliar voice answered. "Blue Wing, may I help you?"

"Yes, this is Lily Raines. I want to check on my father."

"Who's your father?" the woman asked.

Lily frowned. She didn't recognize the voice. "Joe Raines. Who is this?"

"I'm the ward clerk."

The sound of papers rustling crackled through the phone.

"Joe Raines? Would he be under another name?"

Gritting her teeth, Lily answered as calmly as she could. "Try Joseph Raines. Room 118."

"One-eighteen? Nah, that's Mrs. Brown's room."

Lily's heart flip-flopped in her chest. "What? For how long?"

Brand stepped over beside her, concern obvious on his face.

"I'd have to look that up."

"Where is my father?"

"Ma'am, don't raise your voice at me."

Lily gritted her teeth. "I want to know where my father is. Let me speak to the nurse, right now!"

The clerk sighed loudly. "All the nurses are in report. I can have one of them call you."

"I don't want one of them to call me. I want to talk to a nurse, right now."

"If you'll give me your number I'll have them give you a call."

"And you can't tell me anything about Joe Raines? What about his chart?"

"I don't see a chart with that name on it, ma'am. I'm filling in on Blue Wing tonight. I usually work on the Orange Wing."

Her hands shaking so much she could hardly hold the phone, Lily turned to Brand. "What's this number?"

He recited it for her and she gave it to the clerk, then pressed the disconnect button and threw the phone aside. Her eyes burned with the need to cry, but she was too tired, too upset, too frightened.

Brand retrieved the cell phone and pocketed it, then sat beside her. He took her hand. "Pruitt told me he was working on getting your dad to a secure location. I'm sure they picked him up."

"Are you?" she said archly. "How do you know you can trust him? You didn't trust him earlier today."

"Okay. I can't be sure. But Pruitt told me yesterday he was getting a court order. What did the nurse say?"

"All the nurses were in report. I couldn't talk to any of them. The ward clerk *said* she'd have them call me back."

Lily flopped down on the daybed and rubbed her temples, lifted her hair off her neck. "What am I going to do now?" she asked. "My father has disappeared. What if Castellano has him?"

Brand kneeled down beside her and tucked her hand into his. "First thing in the morning, I'll take you to the police. I promise. Then you can see for yourself that your father is safe."

She looked up, startled. "You'd do that? But what about you?"

"I've still got to find out who's been feeding information to Castellano."

"You're convinced someone is."

"Hell, yeah. He knew where I lived. He followed us to the restaurant. And he knew we were meeting Morrison at the casino."

"What about all your issues with the police?"

Brand scowled and rose.

His powerful denim-clad thighs were in Lily's line of sight.

"My issues don't enter into this. Not now. Your safety and your father's is the most important thing. And you're sure as hell not safe with me. The longer this goes on, the more dangerous it's going to get for you."

He retrieved his gun, ejected the magazine and pulled a full one from his pocket. He slapped it into place.

"Where's your weapon?" he asked.

Lily moved to stand. "On the bathroom counter."

"I'll get it." He retrieved the standard issue Glock 9 mm and examined its magazine. It only had two rounds left. He quickly took the last four bullets from his used magazine and inserted them into hers, then slapped it back into place. "Just in case."

He tossed the pistol onto the daybed beside her. "Keep it with you. Now try to get some sleep."

Lily studied him. Strong thighs aside, he was tired, too. He was looking ragged around the edges. The hollows in his cheeks were deeper, as were the lines around his mouth. His blue eyes were dull. "What about you? You're exhausted."

He shook his head. "I'll keep watch."

"The door's locked. We're not going to do more than nap, anyway. We might as well get as much rest as we can."

He searched her face. "I'll sit over here." He held up a hand when she opened her mouth. "And try to nap."

Her gaze traced the tense curve of his shoulders and back that spoke to his exhaustion. He rubbed his face.

Damn, he was stubborn. She sat up and glared at him. "Whatever line you're reluctant to cross, I think we crossed it last night and left it far behind. It won't hurt anything if we lie together just to *sleep.* It's not like we haven't been here before."

His jaw clenched as he stared at her. After a few seconds he pushed a hand through his hair and stood up. "I don't have the strength to do anything but sleep."

"Neither do I. And I feel selfish taking the only bed when you so obviously need rest."

Lily slid toward the wall as he sat down on the bed. He set his gun on the floor within easy reach, then stretched out carefully on the small daybed.

He took up so much space! It was the same as with the tiny studio—he overpowered it with his masculine presence.

He shut his eyes, his long lashes resting against his cheeks. She let herself absorb the sensations created by his closeness. The easy rise and fall of his chest, the hard comfort of his shoulder and bicep against her side, and his long legs.

He turned over with his back to her. Following an impulse she wasn't sure she completely understood, Lily spooned herself against him.

He tensed as she slipped her arm around his waist, but when she didn't do anything else, he relaxed back against her with a sigh.

She closed her eyes and prayed for a few hours of safety.

THEY WERE AFTER HER. They had her father and they were chasing her. She ran as fast as she could, but her legs were like lead weights. She could barely lift them.

Where was Brand? He'd promised to keep her safe, but he was nowhere around. Why had he abandoned her and her father?

She'd thought he was trustworthy. She'd thought he was one of the good guys.

She screamed his name!

"Lily."

The men chasing her dissolved, melted into the hot asphalt beneath her feet.

A strong, protective arm held her tight.

"Lily, wake up. You're having a bad dream."

She opened her eyes and arched her back, prepared to fight.

It was Brand. The yellow light streaming in through the ancient blinds planed his face in eerie shadows.

"Where were you?" she whispered frantically.

"I'm right here. You were dreaming."

"No, they were right behind me. They were catching up. They almost—"

His warm hands framed her face, his thumbs lightly tracing her lips. "Shh. It's okay. It was only a dream."

She closed her eyes. "They had my dad—"

"Shh. Your father's safe, remember? He's in police custody."

The haze of sleep finally left her. She was in the little studio with Brand. Fully awake and achingly aware of Brand's hard body pressed close to hers, Lily nodded carefully. "We don't know that for sure, do we?"

"No, but we will first thing in the morning. Try not to worry. I'm sure he's safe."

She remembered his earlier words. *One of us has to trust the other.* "Okay. I'm sorry." She rested her head against his shoulder.

Brand pressed his lips to her forehead, trying desperately to think of her as nothing more than an innocent citizen in need of his protection. Unfortunately, his body wasn't having any of it.

His arousal pressed painfully against the seam of his jeans. He carefully slid away from her on the narrow bed. He didn't want to frighten her with his desperate, obvious need.

And truthfully, he didn't relish being rebuffed.

She clutched at his T-shirt. "Are you getting up?" she asked in a small voice.

Brand brushed his thumbs across her damp cheeks and turned her face up to his. "I'll be right here," he said, working to keep his voice calm.

She didn't let go of his shirt. "Will you hold me? Please?"

Wincing internally, he nodded and slipped his arm under her. She curled into his side, her head lying in the hollow of his shoulder. Her sweet scent tortured him. Her innocent trust humbled and shamed him. He wasn't worthy. He'd hurt her and put her in danger.

Some protector he was.

He put his hand over hers and gently pried her fingers from the material of his T-shirt. "You're wound tighter than a spring. Look how stiff your fingers are. Relax. Try to sleep."

"I'm afraid I'll have another nightmare."

"Think good thoughts. Concentrate on something pleasant."

She snuggled a bit closer. She was quiet for so long he thought she'd gone to sleep.

"Why did you become a cop?"

Her question came out of nowhere. It surprised him. He took a deep breath of her intoxicating scent, then opened his mouth to give her the pat answer. *To do something good, something meaningful with my life.*

But the canned words wouldn't come.

She was beginning to trust him. Maybe she had a right to know exactly why he'd started on the path that had brought them together in this place and time.

"All my life my pop was a drunk. He was also a carpenter—a good one, when he wasn't drinking. When he was drinking he was a bastard." He heard the bitterness that scraped across his throat.

Lily's fingers entwined with his. Her touch was comforting, caring.

"I had two big brothers. Patrick was eleven years older than me. He went into business with Pop. He wanted to be just like him." He paused and sighed. "He was."

"Patrick drinks?"

He nodded. "He did. And gambled."

"What about your other brother?"

"Ryan? He's four years older. He always took care of me when I was little. Many nights he stood between me and Pop. He tried to stand between Mom and Pop, too, but—" The old memories were still so vivid, the wounds raw and biting.

Lily stayed quiet. He pressed her hand to his chest and turned his head to breathe in her erotic scent.

"You told me earlier that your father just died."

"Last week. He had cirrhosis of the liver, a bad heart, emphysema—you name it."

"I'm really sorry. You said you didn't want to be like him. So did you become a cop to get away from him? From that life?"

He shook his head. "I became a cop because of Patrick. When I was thirteen and Ryan was away at school, I found Patrick on our doorstep. He'd been shot in the head."

Shock registered on Lily's face. "Oh no! Brand! What happened? Who—"

Her voice gave out and she raised a hand to her mouth.

He watched her expression change to horror as the truth dawned. "Castellano?" she whispered.

"Patrick had a dollar bill stuffed in his mouth. Castellano's trademark."

"But why?"

"He owed Castellano a lot of money. Gambling. Castellano knew he'd never be able to pay up, so he made an example out of him."

Lily looked at him quizzically. "And that's why you became a police officer? To avenge your brother's murder?"

He heard the faint note of censure in her voice. Did she realize she was disappointed in him? Maybe not, but he did.

"What did you expect me to say, that I wanted to make the world a better place? Make it safe? Or that I felt I should repay society for my brother and my father's mistakes by doing good deeds?"

Lily looked stunned. She shook her head. "No, I—"

"Come on, Lily. Admit it. You think I'm tarnishing the

badge, don't you? I tried to tell you. Your father may have been one of the good guys, but there aren't that many of them left. Did you really expect me to be one?"

She swiped her fingers across her cheeks. "I'm so sorry about your brother and your father, and the things you had to endure."

Brand sat up, pushing her away. "Don't be. I'm not. What's the saying? *What doesn't kill me makes me strong?* Well, what I lived with made me very strong. Made me sure of what I wanted to do with my life. Kept me from sinking into a bottle like my old man."

"So you sank into bitterness instead?"

He forced a laugh through his tight throat. "I'm not bitter. Just realistic. My family was a far cry from your idealistic childhood—" He stopped when she went rigid and fury turned her eyes black.

He'd gone too far. He didn't want to destroy her memories. He just wanted her to realize how different they were from his.

"Idealistic? You think my life was idealistic? You think I've forgotten how devastated I was when my mother died? How much I needed my father? But he wasn't there for me. He took a leave of absence. For months he sat in the dark day after day because he didn't know how to deal with losing her. You think I don't remember that he wouldn't even look at me because I reminded him of her?"

"Lily, I didn't mean to—"

"You think I wouldn't rather remember my father as the big, strong man who took care of me and my mother, rather than the way he is now? Some days he thinks I'm one of the nurses. He tells me the same things every time I see him, as if I haven't just been there the day before."

Her lower lip trembled and her eyes sparkled with unshed tears.

He wrapped his arm around her again.

She didn't pull away. "We have the ability to choose our memories, to choose what we bring from the life we were born into," she said, sitting up.

He thought she was going to get up, but instead she leaned over and placed her hand in the middle of his chest. She kissed his cheek.

"Your memories are what you make them," she whispered against his ear.

He pressed his forehead to hers, his chest tight with emotion. "I suppose we can always make new memories."

Lily smiled. "I suppose."

He lay down and pulled her with him, nuzzling the soft skin under her chin, running his hand over her shoulders and down her arms, then around her waist and up, to cup her small, firm breasts. His thumb teased the peaks that were clearly outlined under her cotton T-shirt.

With a quiet gasp she sought his mouth.

He rose and held himself above her. Then he smiled and kissed her deeply, intimately, as his arousal sprang to full hardness. He couldn't hide what she did to him.

She opened herself to him, arching upward. As he slipped one hand between them to undo her jeans, she reached for his. Quickly they disposed of their clothing and lay skin to skin.

Lily ran her hands over his steely biceps, his smooth,

sculpted chest, his flat, hard belly. He was so totally, deliciously male. Then, as her body readied itself for his penetration, she touched him, guided him.

He pushed into her, at first slowly, then with growing intensity. She threw her head back with a soft cry.

Fiercely, urgently, he thrust again and again, driving her into a frenzy of sensation. Nothing had ever felt so good. No one had ever coaxed such a primal, wanton response from her body.

She bit his shoulder to keep from screaming as she came. His guttural moan and straining hips told her he was right there with her.

He thrust one final time, shuddering, and lay carefully against her as her body tightened around him in the aftershocks of orgasm.

He rested his head on her shoulder, his quick, sharp breaths warming her skin. She slid her fingers along the nape of his neck, ruffling his hair, breathing in his clean soap-and-mint scent.

Brand's eyes stung. He felt like a schoolboy experiencing the agonies of first love. For the first time in his life he felt a real connection with another person—something far beyond the simple physical couplings that had been his previous experience.

This was different. Lily was different.

During their enforced closeness, she'd learned more about him than he'd ever told anyone. She saw him as he really was. That scared the crap out of him.

He lifted his head and looked down at her. "How're you doing?" he whispered, touching her cheek.

She nodded and kissed him lightly. Her eyes drifted shut. She sighed through parted lips.

He lay beside her and watched her, wondering what he was going to do, now that he'd allowed himself to care for her.

He closed his eyes and drifted to the edge of sleep, feeling more content, more relaxed than he remembered ever feeling before in his life.

The sound of metal sliding against metal shocked him awake.

Someone was trying to unlock the door!

Chapter Eleven

Brand rolled out of bed in one swift motion and grabbed his jeans, pulling them on quickly, then picked up his weapon.

He glanced at his watch. Who would come to an empty studio at two o'clock in the morning?

As he started for the door, he heard Lily stir. He turned, his finger at his lips, warning her to stay quiet. "Get into the bathroom," he whispered.

She stared at him wide-eyed.

"Do it!" he said through gritted teeth.

She grabbed up her jeans and T-shirt and looked around. Brand jerked his head toward the bathroom.

She reached across to an end table and picked up the Glock he'd reloaded for her. Then she rushed into the tiny bathroom.

Brand flattened himself against the wall beside the door, his weapon ready. He heard the jangle of keys.

Could it be a housekeeper? His racing pulse slowed a bit. Did Cassie's building have a cleaning service?

He didn't have time to ponder the answer. The scrape of metal against metal told him whoever was out there had slipped a key into the lock.

He stepped in front of the door, pointing his gun through the wood toward the person on the other side of the panels.

"Who's there?" he yelled gruffly.

He heard a surprised squeal and a jangling crash as a ring of keys hit the floor.

"Who's in there?" a shaky female voice responded. "Nobody's supposed to be in Mrs. Gallagher's studio." The footsteps retreated.

"Wait!" he shouted. It was Housekeeping. He had to make a decision—fast. He sure didn't want the woman calling the police and reporting a break-in.

He unlocked the door and peered out. A young woman with tired eyes stood behind a cleaning cart. She had the keys in one hand and her cell phone in the other, and she was backing away from the door.

"Hi," Brand said, hiding his gun behind the wooden door. He wiped his face and forced a yawn. "I'm Mrs. Gallagher's brother-in-law. I'm staying here for a couple of days while I'm in town."

The young woman eyed him suspiciously, her thumb poised over the phone's buttons.

"I can show you my driver's license, or I could give you her number. You could check with her." He nodded at her cell phone and smiled. "Although it's pretty late."

The young woman wasn't impressed. Her thumb twitched nervously. "What's your name?"

"Brand. Brand Gallagher. My brother is Ryan Gallagher. This studio belongs to my sister-in-law, Cassie." He ran a hand through his hair and smothered another yawn. "She just had a baby."

She looked past him, then met his gaze again. "I'm supposed to clean twice a week."

"Could you skip tonight? I've got an early meeting tomorrow. Need to get some sleep."

She frowned and opened her mouth.

Brand dug in his pocket. "I'd be glad to reimburse you for any trouble." He found a crumpled twenty and offered it.

She squeezed her cell phone in her fist and reached for the bill. "I'll be back on Wednesday. You will be gone?"

"I'll be out of here by then. Thanks." He pushed the door shut and locked it.

She'd agreed easily enough, but his gut told him she hadn't bought his story about the early meeting. He didn't blame her. He wouldn't have bought it, either. He wasn't even sure she believed he was Cassie's brother-in-law.

Would she call the police? She'd hadn't hesitated to yank the twenty out of his fingers. Maybe he should have given her more.

The bathroom door opened with a soft creak.

"So *Brand Gallagher*, who was that? The cleaning service?"

"You heard."

She nodded. "Were you ever going to tell me your real name?"

"My real name is Brand."

"You know what I'm talking about."

He shrugged. "There never seemed to be a good time."

"Right." She'd dressed and pulled her hair back into a ponytail. It made her look like a teenager. "Do you think she's going to call somebody?"

He didn't know. "I don't think so. She's got a lot of offices to clean, and she's already tired."

Lily nodded, not looking at him. "What are we going to do now?"

She was acting like a skittish colt. She'd been lulled, as he had, into a false sense of security in the quiet, cozy studio. In reality Castellano's men were still after her, and he still didn't know who to trust.

"Like I told you, first thing in the morning I'm going to take you to the police."

"What makes you so certain that I'll be safer with the police than with you?"

He spread his hands. "I haven't done such a good job so far. Obviously, I can't keep you safe. As long as you're out here with me, you're exposed. The police can hide you, guard you."

"They could have done that two days ago. Why now? Why are you suddenly eager to get rid of me?"

Damn it, she was stubborn. "Because you're too much of a distraction," he said.

She blinked, then propped her fists on her hips. "So you're going to turn me over to the people you don't trust just to get me out of the way?"

"If that's how you want to look at it."

"You'll be putting me into a virtual prison. I guess I'm supposed to just sit there and wait? While you do what?"

"Keep looking for answers. Try to stop the people who're determined to kill you." He shook his head in regret. "I should have taken you in a long time ago."

Lily assessed the man who'd been her enemy and turned into her rescuer—and much more.

His blue eyes were clouded with doubt. Two deep lines furrowed his brow. She read the worry and regret in his face.

She nodded. "But you didn't."

His gaze faltered. "I'm sorry. I did what I thought was best at the time."

She bit her lip. "I know," she said gently.

Everything he'd done had been to protect her. It was an unfamiliar feeling, having someone else worry about her. It gave her a sense of security she hadn't felt in a very long time.

"What now?"

"I need to check on my lieutenant." He pulled out his cell phone, looked at it and cursed. "There's not much battery power left."

To her surprise, he tossed the phone to her. Then he retrieved the phone book from his sister-in-law's desk.

"Call County General and ask if Gary Morrison is able to talk. Here's the number." He read off a series of numbers and Lily punched them into the phone.

"Tell them you're his sister."

She pressed the call button and spoke to the hospital's switchboard.

"I'm sorry, ma'am. I have no information on a Mr. Morrison."

Lily met Brand's gaze. "But I'm his sister. I just got word he's been injured. Please. I need to speak to him. I have to know if he's all right."

The operator hesitated. "I'm sorry, ma'am. I'm not authorized to give out any information. You should speak with your brother's family."

She disconnected.

"What did they say?"

"The operator finally said she wasn't authorized to give out information. So my guess is he's there, but either the police have him under guard, or—"

"Or he didn't survive."

"Don't think that way."

"I've got to see him. I think Pruitt's right. Morrison knows or suspects who's leaking information to Castellano."

"What are you going to do?"

"Go to the hospital."

"But the police will be waiting for you."

He nodded as he reached for his T-shirt. "Most likely."

"What will they do?"

"Pruitt's already told me he'll have my badge."

"But that's not fair. None of this is your fault."

Brand smiled without humor. "I admire your sudden faith in me, but the brass won't see it that way."

Lily thought about Brand walking into County General and being picked up, possibly even put under arrest, by his fellow officers. "I'll go."

He pulled his T-shirt over his head and smoothed it down over his ribs. "You? No, you won't. The only place you're going is to Pruitt's office to be placed in protective custody."

"No, I can do it. I can walk into the hospital without being noticed. If your lieutenant is there, he'll be guarded, right? I can find out where he is, maybe even talk to his family. I can get them to let you see him."

"That's a great plan, Lily. But it won't work."

"Why not?"

"First of all, if the police are guarding him, it's not going to be his family's choice who gets in to see him. And as you say, as soon as I'm spotted, they'll take me into custody."

"Then I'll get in to see him myself and ask him what he wanted to tell you."

Brand shook his head. "All this is based on the assumption that Morrison is there and able to talk."

"Well, what's *your* plan based on?"

He sent her a sidelong glance as he checked his weapon and slid it into the waistband of his jeans. "Same thing."

She propped her fists on her hips. "Okay then. My way makes more sense."

He shrugged into his shirt, leaving the tail out to hide his gun. "No, it doesn't."

"Yes, it does. Besides, we need to hurry. It will be better if we go during the midnight shift." Lily picked up her gun and slipped it into a zippered tote bag that she picked up off the desk by the door.

He nodded. "Okay."

"Okay?" Lily's heart thumped in surprise. "You're agreeing with me?"

He shrugged as he opened the door a crack to peer out. "It's as good a plan as any."

He gestured for her to precede him through the door. "Let's go. Like you said, it'll be easier on the midnight shift."

Lily glanced around the studio, her gaze lingering on

the tangled sheets on the daybed. Then she slipped through the door.

"Stay behind me," Brand whispered as he locked the studio and pocketed the keys.

"How are we getting to the hospital?"

"It's only about three miles. We'll walk, or hail a cab."

"Brand." Lily caught his wrist as he stepped in front of her.

He patted her hand. "It'll be okay. Don't worry. You'll be in protective custody by morning. You'll get to see your father."

She hesitated, then nodded. It was probably better that he hadn't given her the chance to say what she'd started to say. There was no need to complicate the situation by bringing emotions into it.

Better that he think she was worried about herself and her father.

She followed him down the fire stairs. At the door to the street, he paused.

"Wait here while I check out the area. Watch through the reinforced glass. I'll signal you when it's safe for you to come out."

Lily nodded. "Who do you think—"

"I don't know. Maybe nobody. But it never hurts to be careful."

Brand pushed through the fire door into the parking lot. It had rained earlier, and the streetlights were haloed by the damp mist that hung in the freshly washed air. He breathed in the smells of cool rain and hot asphalt. It was unseasonably warm, and wisps of steam rose from the street.

The gas station across the street from the office building was deserted. Its ugly yellow sign barely penetrated the damp air.

He studied the dark street for a few moments, but nothing moved. Everything was quiet. Not even a breeze was blowing.

Taking a deep breath of the still night air, he turned and gestured to Lily.

She slipped through the fire door and hurried to his side.

"Let's get away from here. It's too dark. Too isolated. We'll follow Highway 90. Stick close."

He stepped out onto the street, his hand poised near the handle of his weapon.

He heard the ricochet of the bullet before he heard the report.

Whirling, he threw himself on top of Lily. They hit the ground together, his arm cradling her head.

"What—oof!"

"Shh!" He raised his head and drew his gun. Where had the shot come from?

The answer came in a volley of gunfire. Brand cringed and tried to spread himself more completely over Lily as bullets sent bits of asphalt shooting into the air and zinged past their ears.

The shots were coming from the direction of the gas station. He should have checked the area more closely. He'd been too anxious to get to the hospital. His carelessness had exposed them—they were sitting ducks.

Brand cast about for shelter. About twenty feet in front of them was a garbage bin. He got his feet under him and hovered in a crouch.

"See the metal bin? Run for it," he said to Lily. "I'll cover you."

The mist was growing heavier. Brand could barely make out dark shapes moving toward them under the garish yellow light.

He lifted Lily and pushed her toward the Dumpster. Her breaths sobbed and caught and her tennis shoes crunched on gravel as she sprinted across the open space.

He was right behind her. He got off a couple of shots in the general direction of the building.

More gunfire erupted all around them. Several rounds ricocheted off the garbage bin and thudded into the asphalt.

A bullet caught the edge of his hip as he dove and rolled.

"Ouch! Crap!" He touched the torn denim and felt the scraped skin. The bullet had barely skimmed his flesh.

"Are you hurt?" Lily cried.

"No. It's nothing. Get down!"

He heard a car engine start up. "They're coming. Can you shoot?"

"Yes!"

Lily was breathless, but her head was high and her jaw was set. She crawled to the side of the Dumpster and crouched, her gun trained in the direction of the car's engine.

"I can't see!"

Brand saw a shadow moving toward them. Two shadows. "Watch the shadows! Here they come. Try to wound them. We don't know whether they're police or Castellano's men."

He was almost certain it wasn't the police. They wouldn't sneak up in dark clothes, taking potshots at them without identifying themselves as law enforcement.

Had Castellano's connections led him to Brand's sister-in-law's studio? Or had someone on the force betrayed him again?

He shot off several rounds, aiming low. He didn't want to kill anyone if he didn't have to.

"Shoot at their feet!" he shouted to Lily.

Helpless fury raged through him. Once again he'd put Lily in danger. He should have turned her over to the police when he had the chance. Now they were trapped.

Castellano wanted her dead, and Brand had delivered her right into the mob boss's hands.

He aimed at a shadow. In the distance he heard a car engine turn over. A black sedan appeared from the darkness behind the gas station. It approached slowly.

He swung his gun, aiming at the vehicle's windshield, although it was probably a waste of a bullet. If the car belonged to Castellano, it probably had bulletproof glass.

Just as he was about to squeeze the trigger, his ears picked up another sound—sirens wailing in the distance. Someone had heard the gunfire and called the police.

Automatic weapons fire sprayed the garbage bin with dozens of rounds.

"Lily! Stay down," he shouted, cringing backward. A quick glance told him her back was pressed against the dirty metal, and she held her gun in both hands, prepared to shoot. She was on the balls of her feet, poised to whirl and fire off several rounds as soon as the volley stopped. Her expression was intense, focused.

Her bravery in the face of possible death awed him.

The sound of a second car engine split the air. He angled

his head to steal a quick glance. A pair of watery headlights sped toward them through the mist. He trained his weapon on the windshield of the new arrival.

More gunfire filled the air. His pulse pounded and his breath rasped in his throat as he struggled to sort out the sounds.

The new car was firing *at* the other vehicle. He heard a startled shout from one of the gunmen.

Who was it? The police in an unmarked car? He wiped mist from his face and aimed his weapon at the newcomer as it screeched to a halt in front of the Dumpster.

Brand pointed his weapon at the passenger window and tightened his finger on the trigger.

The passenger door swung open.

"Brand!"

He blinked at the familiar voice. It was Springer. How had Springer found them?

"Get the hell in here." Springer's driver's window was down. He took potshots at the moving shadows.

Brand heard the dark car's engine rev.

"They're moving in. Let's go!" Springer's voice was shrill with reaction. He ducked as a bullet ricocheted off the top of his car. "Damn it, hurry!"

Brand grabbed Lily's arm. "Come on. Let's go."

"Who—"

He yanked the passenger seat forward and climbed into the back, then pulled the front seat back into position. Lily dove in. Before she even got the door closed Springer gunned the engine and roared away.

Automatic weapons fire pinged the rear of Springer's

car. The undercover officer's hands were white-knuckled on the steering wheel.

"That was close. How the hell are you?" Springer flashed a toothy grin.

"Where did you come from?" Brand shouted. "How'd you know where we were?"

Springer was too busy to answer. He careered around a corner, wheels screeching, then raced up a side street before finally slowing to a more normal pace.

Lily held on as tightly as she could. She hadn't even had a chance to put on her seat belt. Once Springer slowed down, she turned in her seat.

"Are you all right?" she asked Brand. "You got hit, didn't you? Where?"

He frowned. "It's nothing. Caught the edge of my hip."

Her weapon pressed against her side. She pulled it out, ejected the magazine and held it up. "I'm out of ammunition."

"That's okay," he said. "I've got several rounds left."

Springer glanced over at Lily. "You must be the missing juror," he said conversationally. "So you got yourself one who can shoot, Gallagher?"

Lily stared at the undercover cop for a few seconds. He was a chunky guy, maybe midforties, with a receding hairline and an expanding waist. He had a barrel chest and hefty biceps. She remembered Brand saying that the other two undercover cops worked on the docks. This guy looked as if he could hold his own among longshoremen.

"So are you okay, Ms. Raines?" He waggled his eyebrows at her, then gave a sharp chuckle and glanced in the rearview mirror. "Your juror don't talk much," he tossed back over his shoulder.

He knew who she was? Lily supposed she shouldn't be surprised. Brand had said her picture was plastered all over the papers and the television. But the newspaper had withheld her name.

She supposed Springer had her name because he was a police officer.

Still, she turned and sent Brand a questioning look.

"Springer—"

"Okay. Okay. I overheard a couple of Castellano's goons talking about how you'd screwed him over. They said you roughed up Foshee and ran off with the juror. Gio ain't happy. I can tell you that."

"No kidding. He didn't make me as a cop though, did he?"

"Well, I got the idea he figured you weren't just a bouncer." Springer leered at Lily. "Maybe he thinks you went wacko over the chick."

Brand glanced behind him.

Lily followed his gaze, but the damp street was deserted.

"So when I heard them saying they were on their way to check your sister-in-law's place I figured I'd better see if I could intercept you. Looks like I got there just in time."

"How did they know about Cassie's studio?"

Springer shook his head. "Hell if I know. I just work the docks. Castellano don't confide in me."

"I can't wait to find out who ratted me out."

Springer looked at Brand in the rearview mirror. "Yep. That ain't just your problem, either. If Castellano knows you're a cop, it's only a matter of time before he tumbles to Carson and me. I probably screwed myself, anyhow, coming after you."

A police car passed them going in the opposite direction. Springer turned right onto a side street.

"You don't think whoever betrayed me ratted you two out, too?"

Springer shrugged his massive shoulders. "I don't think so. From what I heard, you were set up to take the fall. Foshee was supposed to kill you after he took out the girl."

Lily stared at him. His bald statement brought home to her how close she'd come to being killed.

How many times could she cheat death? First the Cajun with his lethal knife. Then the pug-nosed gunman in the restaurant. Not to mention the bullets she'd been dodging in the casino garage and in the street just now.

Icy fear crawled up her spine as it occurred to her that her luck might run out at any second. The next attack could be fatal.

Springer glanced at her, and apparently read her mind. "Sorry, Sugar, but it's the truth."

Brand grunted. "That doesn't make sense. Why wouldn't he bring me in, force me to tell him more about the operation before killing me?"

Lily listened in stunned awe, her pulse hammering in her ears. She couldn't believe how nonchalantly they were talking about being tortured and killed. Was this the life her father had led?

Springer just shrugged his shoulders.

"Unless—" Brand paused. "Unless he already knew everything he needed to know."

Springer turned right again. Lily squinted, trying to read the street signs. She wasn't sure where they were, but it felt like they were headed back the way they'd come.

As if picking up on her thoughts, Brand asked, "Where are we going?"

Springer nodded in the general direction of the road ahead. "There's a place down near the docks where we can hide out until morning."

"Why don't we go on in to police headquarters? I need to talk to Pruitt as soon as possible, and I want to see Morrison. You heard he got shot?"

Springer nodded. "How's he doing?"

"I don't know. That's where we were headed, to check on him, when we were ambushed. I think Morrison knows who the leak is."

"Oh, yeah? Pruitt didn't tell me that."

Lily noticed an easing of the tension that radiated from Brand. She let herself relax a little, sitting back in her seat. She took a deep, shaky breath, her limbs trembling in a delayed reaction. She'd been so scared.

But now Brand and Springer seemed to have everything under control.

Springer made another turn. They were nearing the shipyards.

"I wonder if Morrison is right."

"About the leak?" Brand shrugged. "I don't know. He's pretty smart."

"Yeah." Springer shifted in his seat and took his right hand off the steering wheel.

He bent over and reached under his seat. Lily glanced

down. To her surprise, he pulled out a large Glock 9 mm without taking his eyes off the road.

"What is it?" she asked. "What's wrong?"

Behind her, Brand sat up. He must have heard the note of alarm in her voice. "What's the matter, Lily?"

Her mouth went dry. All she could do was shake her head.

Springer wrapped his hand around the gun without taking his eyes off the road. "We're almost there."

"Where?" Brand snapped. "This looks like Castellano's place."

Springer pressed the barrel of the gun into Lily's thigh. "You got good eyes, Gallagher. It's the alley behind Gio's. Now listen to me and listen good. You so much as breathe wrong and your girlfriend here loses her leg."

Chapter Twelve

Lily stifled a scream as the gun barrel dug painfully into her flesh.

Brand's fellow officer had betrayed them. She read the shock and fury on his face in the split second it took him to realize what Springer was doing.

He reached for his weapon.

"Hands up, Gallagher!" Springer snapped. The car jerked as his hand tightened on the steering wheel. "Let me see 'em. I'll shoot her leg off, I swear."

Brand grimaced and raised his empty hands. His gaze met hers briefly, warning her not to move. "What the hell's the matter with you, Springer?"

"Don't give me that. Where's your gun? Don't move a muscle. Just tell me."

"It's stuck in the waistband of my jeans. In the middle of my back."

"Then you keep your hands where I can see 'em."

Brand stuck his empty hands up in the air. "I don't get it. What happened to you? You're a good cop. A good man. What about your family?"

Springer laughed. "My family?" he spat. "You want to know what happened to my family? Come on, man. Didn't you notice what happened when you took this job? You were engaged, right? Where's your pretty little fiancée now?"

Brand blinked. "What's that got to do with this?"

Fiancée? The word cut through Lily like a saber. The sharpness of the pain surprised her. Brand had told her he wasn't in a relationship. He'd said it was because of his undercover assignment. She'd believed him. In fact, she hadn't even considered that he might have a past. That showed how naive she was.

Springer was talking. "I had a wife and two kids. I got nothing now. She left me, took the kids back to Dallas, where she grew up. You know why?"

Lily heard the anger and grief in Springer's voice. He was desperate. His chest heaved as the barrel of his gun pushed into her thigh muscle, causing it to cramp.

She cringed and took a deep, shaky breath.

"Do—you—know—why?" Springer yelled.

Brand sat up a little straighter. "Because you were never home?"

"Because even when I was there I wasn't there. That's what *she* said."

Lily looked down at his hand. He was squeezing the gun's handle so hard the barrel shook.

"Now I got nothing. I can't even see my kids. And I'm doing Castellano's dirty work."

"Man, I'm sorry—"

"Shut up! I've got to think." He turned the steering wheel one-handed into the parking lot of Gio's.

The upscale nightclub was located on a side street down near the docks. Its fame had spread by word of mouth over the past twenty years. These days, with the casinos pulling in the Vegas crowds, Gio's was still *the* place for A-list celebrities to relax and party.

Lily had never been there, but like everyone else, she'd heard the stories—the major star who'd died on the dance floor, the shooting one night that left an intern to a famous politician paralyzed.

"So that's how Castellano kept finding us. You've been feeding him information. You knew my brother's name, knew about my sister-in-law's studio."

Springer stopped the car and reached across with his left hand to turn off the key. He moved the gun from Lily's thigh to her ribs. "Tell him where the gun's pointing now, Sugar."

She cringed as he dug the weapon into her side. "It's pointed at my heart."

"That's right, Gallagher. And I'm watching you. Keep those hands up."

"Why did it take so long to ambush us there? Why didn't you move in on us the first night?"

Without bothering to answer him, Springer pulled a cell phone from his shirt pocket and pressed a pre-recorded number. "Yo, Foshee. It's Springer. I've got 'em. Hell, yeah. I told you I would. Come out here and give me a hand."

He half turned toward Brand. "Nah, not yet," he said into the phone.

He paused and Lily heard the Cajun's nasal twang through the phone, although she couldn't understand what he was saying.

"Because Castellano wants to see 'em first. Don't worry, you'll get your chance."

Lily saw the back door of Gio's open. The little Cajun came swaggering out, toying with his knife. A big gun was visible under his jacket and he had a strip bandage across the bridge of his nose.

As he drew closer, she saw that he had a black eye and a cut, swollen lip, too. Brand had done that. She swallowed nervously. The Cajun was going to be out for revenge.

Springer lowered the driver's side window.

"Foshee, watch Gallagher. He's got a gun stuck in his pants."

Foshee walked around to the passenger door. He closed his knife with one hand and drew his gun before opening the car door.

Lily didn't move as the Cajun stuck his head in and grinned at her. "Hello, Lily. You didn't pay attention to me. Dat was a bad mistake. Now you and your boyfriend gotta pay."

He pointed his gun at Brand and grabbed her arm with his left hand. He leaned closer, until his garlicky breath was hot against her cheek. "You try anything and my buddy Brand gets his head blown off. Understand?"

She nodded. Terror stole her breath and paralyzed her limbs. She couldn't move. She was certain of it.

"Come on, Lily." He jerked on her arm, never taking his eyes off Brand.

She tried to rise, but her knees gave out.

Foshee jerked harder, twisting her arm.

She bit her lip against the pain and tried to think, tried to come up with a plan to disarm the Cajun, but her brain wouldn't work. All she could think of was his big gun aimed right at Brand's head.

She swung her quivering legs out of the car and stood, certain she was going to crumple. Her hand went to the door to steady herself.

Foshee shoved her away from the door, hanging on to her arm and keeping Brand covered.

He knew who the real threat was. Lily felt helpless, impotent against Foshee and Springer and their guns. Even if she tried to create a diversion, she knew Foshee would make good on his threat. He'd shoot Brand first.

"Get out," he snarled at Brand. "And keep your hands up. If you drop 'em, I drop you. Springer, watch his back."

Brand placed both hands on the seat back, pushed it forward and climbed out of Springer's car. He kept his hands in full sight of both men at all times.

Lily met his gaze as he straightened, his hands still held up in front of him. He gave a quick shake of his head. She knew exactly what he was saying.

Don't try anything.

Springer rounded the car and shoved Brand up against it.

"Spread 'em." He took Brand's gun, then patted him down.

Brand's fists clenched against the car's metal roof.

"Let's go," Foshee said as Springer finished his search. "Mr. Castellano wants to see you both."

As soon as Springer let him move, Brand glanced over at Lily. She looked small and terrified, with Foshee's skinny arm wrapped around her and his big 9 mm pointed at the back of her neck.

Springer nudged him with his gun. "Get a move on, Gallagher. Walk to the back door. Keep those hands up. You heard Foshee. Make a wrong move and his itchy trigger finger will jerk."

"Oops!" Foshee said, then cackled.

Brand cringed.

"It almost jerked right then, just looking at your lying face, *bioque*."

Brand sent the Cajun a lethal glare, then turned toward the back door to Giovanni Castellano's exclusive club.

He had no clue how to get out of this. More importantly, he had no idea how to get Lily out of it. He should have realized the leak was one of his fellow undercover officers.

But he'd trusted them because they were on the side of the good guys. They'd taken the same oaths as he had. They'd become cops for the same reason he had. To right the wrongs in the world. Or at least that's what he'd assumed.

"How did you know we were meeting with Morrison?" he asked Springer.

The cop nudged him in the back with his gun barrel. "Move it."

Brand walked faster.

At the door, Springer stopped. "You always were his pet. We figured you'd try to contact him, so we kept an eye on him. Pruitt had the same idea, because Morrison's street was crawling with unmarked cars. When he headed to the casinos, it was pretty obvious he was going to meet you. Morrison's no gambler. So we had him followed."

"So it *was* Castellano's men who shot him."

"Sure. I don't know what he'd found out, but we couldn't

take the chance. We had to take him out, so he couldn't tip you off. Then we waited for you two to show up."

He pushed the gun barrel into Brand's side. "Open the door."

Brand knew Castellano was never surprised. The door, which led into the kitchen, would be covered by armed guards. Castellano was very careful about safety—particularly his own.

Sure enough, standing inside the kitchen were two men in dark suits holding automatic weapons under their arms.

Behind him Lily made a small, hurt noise. He turned but Springer dug the gun barrel into his side.

"Don't get worried about your girlfriend, Gallagher. Foshee is taking good care of her."

Brand's whole body tensed in fury. If the Cajun laid one hand on her, Brand would make him pay. Even if it cost Brand his own life.

They passed through the kitchen, which smelled like tomato sauce and freshly baked bread, and entered the dimly lit main rooms of the restaurant.

Over in the far corner, away from the bandstand and close to the exit to his offices, at the table that was always kept reserved for him, Castellano sat. He was surrounded by two of his bodyguards and kept company by two beautiful women.

They were all in evening attire, although it had to be five o'clock in the morning. Brand figured they hadn't gone to bed yet.

Castellano had a glass half filled with amber liquid in front of him. As Springer and Foshee pushed them toward his table, he lifted the glass. His eyes were puffy and heavy-lidded with lost sleep, but he grinned broadly.

"Ah, my trusted employee, Jake Brand. How nice to see you." Castellano saluted him with his drink, then turned it up. "And Ms. Raines. Such a lovely, disobedient little juror. Please, take a seat. I want to try and understand why you couldn't follow simple instructions."

Lily didn't move. Her fists were clenched at her sides and her face was a pale oval in the dim light.

"I said have a seat," Castellano repeated harshly.

Foshee shoved her roughly into a leather chair and stood behind it, his gun pointed at the back of her neck.

Brand's muscles contracted in impotent rage. Castellano was going to toy with her and then, with a nod of his head, her fate would be sealed. She would die, and her death wouldn't be easy.

"Brand, you, too. Come now. We're civilized here."

Springer's gun dug into his ribs. Brand sat in the chair next to Lily. She didn't look up.

His heart ached with searing regret and a lump clogged his throat. He saw in her eyes that she knew he couldn't save her. He longed to touch her, to reassure her, but he didn't have any reassurance for her.

How could he have trusted Springer? He'd been so careful up until that point. But Castellano's gunmen were closing in on them, and Springer was a cop, after all.

Lily's question echoed in his memory. *How can you not trust your fellow officers?*

Too late, he realized that was his fatal flaw.

As cautious and suspicious as he'd been, when it came down to it, he didn't hesitate to trust Springer. Deep down, he did believe the police were the good guys.

"Ms. Raines." Castellano's voice was harsh.

Lily jumped, and Foshee put his hand on her shoulder. She cringed.

"Aren't you going to answer me?"

Lily lifted her chin. "Wh-what was the question?"

Brand hid a smile. She was terrified, yet she refused to give the crime boss the satisfaction of hearing her plead for her life.

While Castellano's attention was on Lily, Brand let his gaze roam over the room, taking in everything and everyone around them, searching for a way out. Their table was equidistant from the front and rear doors of the restaurant.

Behind and to the left was a door that Brand knew led to a private office. He'd never been in there, so he had no idea if there was an exit, but judging by the care Castellano took for his own safety, Brand was sure the King of the Coast wouldn't let himself be trapped in his own office. There had to be an exit.

Brand gauged the distance to the door as Castellano questioned Lily.

"Why did you vote to convict my dear friend Theodore Simon?"

Lily moistened her lips as she deliberately relaxed her hands and flexed her fingers. "He was guilty, Mr. Castellano."

Despite the gravity of their predicament, Brand's heart

swelled in admiration and pride. Lily was gutsy, there was no doubt about that.

Castellano's face turned red. "That's entirely beside the point. I asked you to do me a simple favor and vote not guilty. The jury wouldn't have had a unanimous verdict, a mistrial would have been declared and my friend would have been freed. It was a fine plan."

"Fine for you, maybe. Not for me." Lily's voice quavered slightly. "As soon as the jury was dismissed, you planned to kill me."

Castellano waved his hand. "Why in the world would I do that?"

Lily didn't bother answering.

He laughed. "I like you, Ms. Raines. You've got moxie. It took a lot of courage to do what you did—to vote to convict even though by doing so you caused the death of an innocent man."

Brand saw Castellano's words find their target in Lily's heart. He knew how much Bill Henderson's death weighed on her conscience.

"It's a shame you can't work for me."

"I suppose it is."

At the sound of the door from the kitchen swinging shut, Castellano looked up. "Ah, here's the rest of our party."

It was Carson, the other member of their undercover team. He was led in at gunpoint by a muscle-necked goon. He looked confused and frightened.

"Mr. Carson, welcome to our little party."

Carson looked at Springer, at Brand, then at Castellano. "I don't understand."

The mob boss took a sip of his drink. "No, of course you don't. But you will." He caught Springer's eye and nodded.

"Get up." Springer nudged Brand in the back of his neck with the gun barrel. At the same time, Foshee grabbed Lily's arm and jerked her out of her seat.

Brand met Carson's gaze.

Carson looked at the gun Springer held. "Springer, what the hell—?"

"Mr. Carson, I regret to inform you that your little undercover operation is over. Your trusted friend Mr. Springer has decided to work for me."

"Springer? Why you dirty—" Carson's face turned red and he lunged toward Springer, but the man guarding him coldcocked him with the barrel of his gun.

Carson dropped to the floor with a grunt, then dragged himself to his hands and knees.

The guard nudged him with his foot. "Get up!" He grabbed the back of Carson's shirt and hauled him to his feet.

Lily watched the brutality in horrified amazement. She glanced at Brand and saw anger, frustration and fear cross his face. Her heart sank. She knew what he was thinking. They were hopelessly outnumbered. They were all going to die here.

She longed to reach out and take his hand, to feel his strength, his caring, once more before she died. But even as the thought entered her mind, Foshee dragged her farther away from him.

"Take them away," Castellano said. "You know what to do. Just make sure you dispose of them far enough out in the Gulf that they'll never be found."

Brand's gaze caught Lily's. In that split second, she saw the secrets of his heart reflected in his clear blue eyes. He loved her. Her heart soared.

But then his jaw tightened and her insides clenched with fear. He was going to make a move.

Because he loved her, he would sacrifice his life for her.

No! she wanted to shout. *Please don't make me watch you die.*

Springer's weapon was aimed directly at Brand's head. No matter what he tried, he'd be too slow. Springer would kill him.

Lily stared at Brand then slowly, deliberately, she rolled her eyes back in her head and collapsed, boneless, to the floor.

All hell broke loose.

Foshee jerked on her arm.

Brand dove over the table toward Castellano.

Springer took aim at Brand but hesitated, probably because Castellano was in his line of fire.

Carson head-butted his guard, whose gun went off.

Lily cringed at the report, but the bullet didn't hit her, and she didn't hear anyone cry out in pain. All she heard were the screams of the two young women who had been sitting with Castellano.

The table splintered under the weight of Brand and Springer as they struggled for Springer's gun. Castellano shrieked.

Foshee let go of Lily's arm and moved to help Springer with Brand. Lily grabbed his leg, but he kicked her away.

She saw two more dark-suited men heading their way.

The armed guards from the kitchen. There was no way they'd get out of this alive.

Then suddenly doors crashed open. Light streamed in.

"Stop! Police!"

Lily's heart crashed against her chest.

"Hold it! Nobody move!"

"Drop that gun!"

"Get on the floor! On the floor! Now!"

Lily plastered herself against the carpeted floor. Her pulse pounded in her ears. Her whole body burned with terror. She figured her best bet was not to move.

She heard several shots and more shouts.

Somebody fell on top of her. Was it Foshee? She felt the sticky warmth of blood seeping through the back of her T-shirt.

Then another body crashed down next to her. She lifted her head. It was Springer. His face was frozen in a mask of horror. Was he dead?

It seemed like dozens of pairs of shoes scrambled around her. She closed her eyes and put her hands over her head.

Suddenly, beefy arms wrapped around her and dragged her along the floor.

Kicking and thrashing, she struggled to get away, but the man who held her was too strong. He dragged her through a doorway and kicked it shut behind him.

Lily swung her arms wildly, straining to draw enough breath into her lungs to scream.

"Shut up or I'll shoot you now!"

It was Springer. Blood streamed down the side of his face, the dark red emphasizing the traitor cop's paleness.

She looked down the dark barrel of his massive gun. "Get up. *Get up!*"

Lily was disoriented. She didn't know where they were. It was a dark, stuffy corridor that smelled like whiskey.

As she tried to get her feet under her, Springer grabbed her by the waist and dragged her across the carpeted floor. He wrapped his arm under hers as he shoved a door open with his shoulder and pulled her outside.

Dawn was just breaking, turning everything a faint purple, Lily noticed as Springer yanked her up against his body. He pressed the gun barrel to the back of her head.

She closed her eyes and held her breath, waiting for the shot she knew she wouldn't hear.

BRAND LAUNCHED HIMSELF across the splintered table and grabbed Castellano.

"My leg!" The mob boss screamed. "My leg's broken. Get off me."

Brand had no sympathy for him. His neck stung. He was pretty sure a bullet had dug a furrow into his flesh, but he hadn't had a chance to check it. He'd been too busy scuffling with Springer and too anxious to get his hands on Castellano.

He wasn't quite sure what had happened, but the place was swarming with FBI Task Force jackets. Someone had tipped them off, and none too soon.

He wondered who.

Suddenly, everything went quiet. The gunfire stopped. The lawmen seemed to have everything under control.

"Gallagher!"

It was Pruitt.

Brand sat up, still holding Castellano in a headlock.

"You—Dawson," Pruitt yelled at an officer. "Take Mr. Castellano into custody."

Pruitt knelt next to Brand. "You can let go now, Gallagher. Dawson has him."

Brand relaxed and looked at Pruitt. "Nice of you to come," he said hoarsely. "You got a pair of cuffs for me?"

Pruitt shook his head. "Not today. Morrison woke up. He told me he suspected Springer of turning. Said Springer had come to him a few weeks ago. Asked him to intervene— get him extracted. Said his wife was going to leave him."

Brand nodded. It made sense. "Springer worked under Morrison about the same time I did. Morrison was like a father to us both. What did the lieutenant tell him?"

"What he should have. To see me."

"But Springer didn't. So Morrison was trying to warn me that Springer might be the leak."

Pruitt nodded. "I wish he'd come to me first."

Brand didn't respond to Pruitt's comment. "How'd you and the cavalry get here just in time?"

"I put a tail on Springer as soon as Morrison told me what he suspected. The tail hung back during the gunfight, waiting to see what Springer was going to do. Then when Springer picked up you two, he followed you here and called for backup."

The FBI agent sighed. "Look, Gallagher. I know you and Morrison had your doubts about me, but I had to look at the big picture."

Brand didn't want to hear about Pruitt's big picture. He needed to find Lily.

His gaze swept the room. Where was she? He didn't see her anywhere. Concern ripped through him like a stray bullet. He straightened, ignoring the blood that trickled down his neck. "Where's Lily?"

"I don't know. One of the officers may have taken her outside to be checked by the paramedics."

Brand pushed himself to his feet. He swayed, feeling light-headed. "Lily!"

The restaurant was still swarming with police and FBI agents. But he didn't see a little sparkly white T-shirt anywhere.

"Damn it. Where is she? Lily!" he shouted.

"We'll find her. You need to let the paramedics look at that neck."

"Later. Give me a gun." He grabbed the nearest officer and held out his hand. "Your weapon—now!"

The officer looked at Pruitt, who nodded.

Weapon in hand, Brand turned and pushed through the door in back of Castellano's table. He found himself in a dimly lit corridor with several closed doors leading off it.

The door at the end of the corridor was ajar. He rushed toward it and slammed it open. He was in the parking lot of Gio's. And directly in his line of sight stood Springer, holding Lily with a gun to her head.

Brand's heart jumped into his throat. He could barely get breath enough to speak.

"Springer! Don't do it!" He aimed his gun at Springer's head. He felt his arm muscle quiver. God, he hoped he didn't have to shoot. He was so shook up that he was afraid he might hit Lily.

"Get out of here, Gallagher. I don't want to shoot you."

"You don't want to shoot anybody." Brand's heart pounded. His blood ran cold in his veins. He prayed he could stop Springer. How would he live if Lily died?

He caught her eye.

She was terrified. Her face was white and pinched. She gripped Springer's arm with both hands. Her paleness told Brand she was about to collapse.

Hang in there, Lily.

He turned his attention back to the desperate cop. "You haven't killed anybody yet, have you?"

"What the hell difference does that make? I might as well have. There's nothing left for me."

The defeated tone in Springer's voice worried Brand. It sounded like he'd already given up. If that was true, then Lily's life was in the hands of a man who had nothing to live for.

Brand's pulse thrummed rapidly and his gun barrel wavered. "Let her go. We'll talk. I'll testify for you. Tell 'em you didn't have a choice."

Springer shook his head. "That won't change anything. I'm screwed. Got nothing to go back to. My family's gone. I've lost my pension."

He tightened his grip on Lily. Her brown eyes flashed with fear.

"Don't add murder to it. Don't take an innocent life." He heard his voice quaver. If Lily died—

"Come on. Give me the gun." Brand held out his hand and took a step closer without lowering his gun.

Springer stiffened. His eyes darted back and forth.

Brand went still. "Okay." He raised his outstretched hand in a show of surrender. "Okay. Here's what we'll do. You let Lily go, and I'll stay out here with you. We'll figure something out. How's that?"

Springer's gaze wavered. His arm loosened a bit.

Lily swallowed and stared at Brand.

"Yeah. That's right. Let Lily go. Then you and me, we'll go to Pruitt and talk. Figure out what we can do."

Springer squeezed his eyes shut for an instant, then turned the gun from Lily's head to point at Brand.

"What we can do? There's nothing you or anybody else can do. I'm a dead man."

Brand's mouth went dry. He wasn't going to let her go.

"Come on, man. You don't want to die. We've got Castellano. You'll get consideration for the job you did undercover."

Lily hadn't taken her eyes off Brand. They burned into his skin, but he couldn't risk even a glance at her. He had to watch Springer every second.

She took a shaky breath.

Springer's gun hand shook. He took a long, shuddering breath. "I can't, Gallagher. It's too late."

His arm tightened and Lily gasped.

Brand aimed at Springer's head.

Suddenly, Springer loosened his hold on Lily and pushed her toward Brand, still aiming his gun at Brand's chest.

"There!" he shouted. "Take her. You're blowing smoke. She's all you really want, isn't she? You'd promise me anything in exchange for her life."

Brand did his best to hold his gun hand steady as he

reached out and snagged Lily by the waist. "Springer, let's talk. I've got Lily now and I still want to help you."

Springer put his other hand on his gun. "I can't—"

A shot rang out.

Lily's whole body spasmed.

Shock slashed through Brand with the suddenness of heat lightning. Had Lily been shot?

Chapter Thirteen

"Lily!" God, no! Brand pulled her closer, praying she was all right.

Springer's face registered surprise as he stared at a point over Brand's shoulder. Then his eyes glazed over, the gun dropped from his hand and he crumpled to the ground.

Brand stared at the fallen cop, his brain slowly realizing that it was Springer who'd been shot, not Lily. She'd collapsed in shock and fear.

Holding her close against him, he looked over his shoulder in time to see Pruitt lower his weapon.

"Pruitt! My God!" His whole body tingled with shock and outrage. He loosened his hold on Lily. "Can you stand?" he asked her.

She was white as a sheet, but she nodded.

"Stay here."

Rushing over, he knelt beside Springer's body. "Pruitt. You shot him!"

"He was going to shoot you."

"You don't know that! He'd let Lily go." He turned the fallen cop over. Springer's eyes fluttered.

"Hang in there, buddy. The paramedics are here."

"He had his weapon pointed right at you."

"Get the paramedics!" Brand yelled.

As if they'd heard him, two EMTs ran around the corner of the restaurant. They bent over Springer.

"Step back, sir."

"We've got him. Please give us some room to work."

Brand stood and moved away.

Lily walked up beside him.

"Come on. You two need to be looked at, too." Pruitt barely glanced at Springer as he guided Brand and Lily around to where the squad cars were parked.

He instructed one of his officers to find an EMT to examine them. When the med-tech came rushing over, Brand held up a hand.

"Lily, you go. I need to talk to Pruitt about something."

She sent him a questioning look. "But your neck. You're bleeding."

He nodded encouragingly. "Go ahead. I'll be there in a couple of minutes."

Lily let the EMT lead her toward one of the ambulances.

Brand turned to Pruitt. "What about her father?"

Pruitt sent him a disgusted look. "I told you I'd take care of it."

"Well, did you? Where is he? I hope to hell you picked him up, because he's not at the nursing home."

"Give me some credit, Gallagher. Of course we picked him up. As soon as we got the court order. He's in a guarded room at County General."

Brand breathed a sigh of relief. "Thanks. When we called

the nursing home, the ward clerk had no clue what had happened to him." He turned toward the ambulance.

"Gallagher."

He stopped and turned halfway around. "Yeah?"

"It was a good shoot. Springer was about to pull the trigger."

Brand shook his head. "No shooting is good."

Pruitt had the grace to grimace and nod.

"Anyhow, good job. Thanks to you and Juror Number Seven, we should be able to put Castellano away for a long time."

Brand angled his head and eyed Pruitt with suspicion. He still didn't like the guy, but he trusted him more than he had at first. He sent the FBI agent a short nod, then headed for the ambulance.

The EMT bandaged Brand's neck. He'd already determined that Lily had no injuries.

"All this blood is the Cajun's," she told him. "He fell on me when he was shot."

Brand didn't protest when the EMT put them in the backseat of a squad car to await transport to the central task force location to give their statements.

He sat there for a minute, trying to wipe the image of Lily with a gun to her head out of his mind. But it wouldn't disappear. Nor could he rid himself of the sight of Springer collapsed on the ground, blood blossoming from the wound in his chest.

Lily sighed.

He roused himself. "Pruitt told me they picked up your father."

A muffled sob escaped from her throat. "Oh! I'm so glad. Where is he?"

"At County General, in a guarded room. If you want, I'll take you to see him later today, when we finish giving our statements."

"Thank you. That would be wonderful."

Brand nodded.

They fell silent.

He stared at the flashing blue lights as his brain picked over everything that had happened in the past twenty-four hours.

He tried desperately to figure out how and when he could have handled things differently, but every scenario played out the same way. Either Lily died, or someone else did.

Where had he gone wrong?

LILY FELT THE TURMOIL inside Brand. She wanted to take his hand and comfort him. She longed to reassure him that he'd done everything he could, and that Springer's shooting wasn't his fault.

Two men came around the side of the building carrying a stretcher. The figure on the stretcher was encased in a body bag.

Brand watched until the stretcher was loaded into an ambulance and the doors were closed, then he looked down at his hands.

"It wasn't your fault."

He didn't say anything or move, but she felt him withdraw.

"You did everything you could. You saved my life."

He shook his head.

"You did. You are the bravest, most honorable man I've

ever known. You've been rescuing me and keeping me safe ever since that first night."

Lily's heart felt torn in two. She knew Brand didn't trust love. It had been a long time since she had. But the past few days had reminded her of how unselfish, how generous love was supposed to be.

And how fulfilling.

Brand was afraid of giving his heart, and he had ample reason. Yet she'd seen over and over the proof of his enormous capacity for love. His loyalty to his family, his concern for her and her dad. Even his heartache at the death of the fellow officer who had betrayed him.

She'd felt it in his kiss and in his gentle yet fierce lovemaking.

He hadn't been capable of hiding his goodness and integrity, not even behind a bad-guy facade.

She'd come to know him well in the brief time they'd been forced to rely on each other. She knew he was one of the good guys.

But she also knew that if she let him go tonight, she would never see him again. He might never be able to make the first move. He'd had too much hurt in his life.

Hesitating, she reached for his hand and squeezed his fingers with hers.

"Brand, tell me how you feel. Please." She heard her voice break.

For a moment he sat stiff, rigid. Then he slipped his hand out of her grasp and reached for the car door.

Her heart shattered. He couldn't do it. He couldn't open up.

She swallowed. "Don't go."

He pulled up on the door handle until it clicked open.

A huge lump grew in Lily's throat, making it hard for her to breathe. She bit her lip in an effort to keep tears from gathering.

He tensed, and she waited for him to push the door open and get out of the car. She steeled herself to watch him walk away.

After what seemed like an eternity, he let go of the handle and without raising his head he held out his hand.

She took it.

"I don't understand love," he said quietly. "Why people want it. It hurts. It bleeds. It destroys." He took a breath. "Look at Springer. He loved his wife and children, but she left him and took his kids away, and it ended up killing him."

His fingers tightened. "Look at my family. We're champions at hurting each other. Always have been." He stopped.

"It doesn't have to be like that."

His head jerked as if in response to a blow. "How the hell would you know? Your husband betrayed you in the worst way."

"I don't believe everyone is like him. I believe there are genuinely good people in the world. People worthy of great love. I believe true love can be wonderful."

He was silent for a moment, but he didn't let go of her hand. "What I've found out these last few days is that trying not to love hurts even more." His head bent over their clasped hands.

Lily tried not to rejoice at his words. She had no idea what he was going to say.

She gazed at his dark, tousled hair, at his vulnerable nape, at the trickle of blood drying on his neck. His silky hair and the fine shape of his head made her throat hurt.

It was a moment before he spoke again. "You've been very brave. But I've got to know. Just how brave are you, Lily Raines?" He raised his head. "Are you brave enough to try life with a man who knows nothing about love?"

Lily couldn't move. She was stunned. Had she really heard right? Was he asking her for a lifetime commitment?

Slowly, her mouth stretched in a huge smile. She leaned over and placed her palm against his cheek and turned his head until he looked into her eyes.

"I don't think there's a woman on the planet who's that brave. But thank goodness I don't have to worry about that. The man I love and want to live my life with knows all about love."

Brand's blue eyes sparkled. "You think so?" he asked hoarsely.

She kissed him gently on the lips. "I know so. But if he doesn't mind, I sure would like to hear him say it."

His eyes softened and he smiled. "Say what?"

"I love you."

"Oh, that. I love you, Lily Raines."

He loved her. Her heart soared with joy. "I love you, too, Brand Gallagher—if that *is* your real name."

Brand laughed and lifted her hand to his lips. "Brandon Christopher Gallagher. That's all of it." He kissed each knuckle then turned her hand over and kissed the palm.

"I don't know why you love me, Lily, but I'm grateful that you do."

"You don't know why?" She looked deep into his blue eyes. "I'd have thought you'd figured that one out by now," she said. "It's obvious, Brandon Christopher Gallagher. You're one of the good guys."

* * * * *

We hope you enjoyed JUROR NO. 7 by Mallory Kane.
You can also give the gift of romance to others.
See page 250 to find some ideas for sharing your books,
and make someone feel as special as you do.

Look for Mallory Kane's next book,
HIGH SCHOOL REUNION, on sale from
Harlequin Intrigue in December 2008.
Then watch for HIS BEST FRIEND'S BABY
by Mallory Kane, the first of three books in the thrilling
new trilogy BLACK HILLS BROTHERHOOD,
on sale in September 2009.
Six passionate and spine-tingling romances are
available from Harlequin Intrigue each month, wherever
books are sold, including most bookstores,
supermarkets, discount stores and
drugstores.

*Harlequin Intrigue is breathtaking romantic suspense.
Because the best part of every great romance is the
mystery...
Enjoy a sneak preview of
SECRETS IN FOUR CORNERS by Debra Webb,
on sale in January 2009, book one
in the heart-stopping continuity,*
KENNER COUNTY CRIME UNIT,
available through September 2009!

Chapter One

Sabrina Hunter fastened her utility belt around her hips. "Eat up, Peter, or we're gonna be late."

Peter Hunter peered up at his mom, a spoonful of Cheerios halfway to his mouth. "We're always late."

This was definitely nothing to brag about. "But," his mother reminded him, "our New Year's resolution was to make it a point *not* to be late anymore." It was only January twelfth. Surely, they weren't going to break their resolution already.

Chewing his cereal thoughtfully, Peter tilted his dark head and studied her again. "Truth or dare?"

Bree took a deep breath, reached for patience. "Eat. There's no time for games." She tucked her cell phone into her belt. Mondays were always difficult. Especially when Bree had worked the weekend and her son had spent most of that time with his aunt Tabitha. She spoiled the boy outrageously, as did her teenage daughter, Layla. Even so, Bree was glad to have her family support system when duty called, as it had this weekend.

Peter swallowed, then insisted, "Truth. Is my real daddy a jerk just like Big Jack?"

Bree choked. "Where did you hear something like that?"

"Cousin Layla said so." He nodded resolutely. "Aunt Tabitha told her to hush 'cause I might hear. Is it true? Is my real daddy a jerk?"

"You must've misunderstood, Peter." *Breathe.* Bree moistened her lips and mentally scrambled for a way to change the subject. "Grab your coat and let's get you to school." Memories tumbled one over the other in her head. Memories she had sworn she would never allow back into her thoughts. That was her other New Year's resolution. After eight years it was past time she'd put *him* out of her head and her heart once and for all.

What the hell was her niece thinking, bringing *him* up? Particularly with Peter anywhere in the vicinity. The kid loved playing hide and seek, loved sneaking up on his mother and aunt even more. His curious nature ensured he missed very little. Tabitha and Layla knew this!

Bree ordered herself to calm down.

"Nope. I didn't misunderstand." Peter pushed back his chair, carefully picked up his cereal bowl and headed for the sink. "I heard her."

Bree's pulse rate increased. "Layla was probably talking about…" Bree racked her brain for a name, someone they all knew—anyone besides *him.*

Before she could come up with a name or a logical explanation for her niece's slip, Peter turned to his mother once more, his big blue eyes—the ones so much like his father's and so unlike her brown ones—resolute. "Layla said my real daddy—"

"Okay, okay." Bree held up her hands. "I got that part." How on earth was she supposed to respond? "We can talk on the way to school." Maybe that would at least buy her some time. And if she were really lucky Peter would get distracted and forget all about the subject of his father.

Something Bree herself would very much like to do.

Thankfully her son didn't argue. He tugged on his coat and picked up his backpack. So far, so good. She might just get out of this one after all. Was that selfish of her? Was Peter the one being cheated by her decision to keep the past in the past? Including his father?

Bree pushed the questions aside and shouldered into the navy uniform jacket that sported the logo of the Towaoc Police Department. At the coat closet near her front door, she removed the lockbox from the top shelf, retrieved her service weapon and holstered it. After high school she'd gotten her associate's degree in criminal justice. She hadn't looked back since, spending a decade working in reservation law enforcement. The invitation to join the special homicide task force formed by the Bureau of Indian Affairs and the Ute Mountain Reservation tribal officials had been exactly the opportunity she had been looking for to further her career.

Besides her son and family, her career was primary in her life. Not merely because she was a single parent, either, although that was a compelling enough motive. She wanted to be a part of changing the reservation's unofficial reputation as the murder capital of Colorado. This was her home. Making a difference was important to her.

Not to mention work kept her busy. Kept her head on straight and out of that past she did not want to think about, much less talk about.

No sooner had she slid behind the wheel of her SUV and closed the door had Peter demanded, "Truth, Mommy." He snapped his safety belt into place.

So much for any hopes of him letting the subject go. She could take the easy way out and say his aunt and cousin were right. His curiosity would be satisfied and that would be the end of that—for now anyway. But that would be a lie. There were a lot of things she could say about the man who'd fathered her child, but that he was bad or the kind of jerk her ex, Jack, had turned out to be definitely wasn't one of them.

"Your father was never anything like Big Jack." Even as she said the words, her heart stumbled traitorously.

"So he was a good guy?"

Another question that required a cautiously worded response. "A really good guy."

"Like a superhero?"

Maybe that was a stretch. But her son was into comics lately. "I guess you could say that." Guilt pricked her again for allowing the conversation to remain in past tense…as if his father were deceased. Another selfish gesture on her part.

But life was so much easier that way.

"Am I named after him?"

Tension whipped through Bree. That was a place she definitely didn't want to go. Her cell phone vibrated. Relief flared. "Hold on, honey." Bree withdrew the phone from the case on her belt and opened it. "Hunter."

"Detective Hunter, this is Officer Danny Brewer."

Though she was acquainted with a fair number of local law enforcement members, particularly those on the reservation, the name didn't strike a chord. "What can I do for you, Officer Brewer?"

"Well, ma'am, we have a situation."

His tone told her far more than his words. *Something.*

When she would have asked for an explanation, he went on, "We have a one eighty-seven."

Adrenaline fired in Bree's veins. Before she could launch the barrage of homicide-related questions that instantly sprang to mind, Brewer tacked on, "My partner said I should call you. He would've called himself but he's been busy puking his guts out ever since we took a look at the...vic."

Damn. Another victim.

Bree blinked, focused on the details she knew so far. Puking? Had to be Officer Steve Cyrus. She knew him well. Poor Cyrus lost his last meal at every scene involving a body.

One eighty-seven.

Damn.

Another murder.

"Location?" Bree glanced at her son. She would drop him off at school and head straight to the scene. Hell of a way to start a Monday morning.

"The Tribal Park." Brewer cleared his throat. "In the canyon. One of the guides found the victim."

"Don't let him out of your sight," Bree reminded. She

would need to question the guide at length. Chances were he would be the closest thing to a witness, albeit after the fact, she would get. "Did you ID the victim?"

Bree frowned at the muffled conversation taking place on the other end of the line. It sounded like Brewer was asking his partner what he should say in answer to her question. Weird.

"Ma'am," Brewer said, something different in his voice now, "Steve said just get here as fast as you can. He'll explain the details then."

When the call ended Bree stared at her phone then shook her head.

Damned weird.

"M-o-o-o-m," Peter said, drawing out the single syllable, "you didn't answer my question."

She definitely didn't have time for that now. "We'll have to talk later. That was another police officer who called. I have to get to work."

Peter groaned, but didn't argue with her. He knew that for his mom work meant something bad had happened to someone.

As Bree guided her vehicle into the school's drop-off lane, she considered her little boy. She wanted life on the reservation to continue to improve. For him. For the next generation, period. As hard as she worked, at times it never seemed to be enough.

"Have a good day, sweetie." She smoothed his hair and kissed the top of his head.

His cheeks instantly reddened. "Mom."

Bree smiled as he hopped out of the SUV and headed

for Towaoc Elementary's front entrance. Her baby was growing up. Her smile faded. There would be more questions about his father.

She couldn't think about that right now.

Right now she had a homicide to investigate.

SOMETIME LATER, BREE sighed as she caught sight of the official Ute Reservation police SUV. A beat-up old pickup, probably belonging to the guide, was parked next to the SUV.

Another murder.

The idea that Steve Cyrus wanted her on the scene before he passed along any known details nagged at her again. What was with the mystery?

She parked her vehicle, grabbed a pair of latex gloves from her console and climbed out.

As if her instincts had picked up on something in the air, her pulse rate quickened.

"Hunter," Steve Cyrus called out as he headed in her direction. "I need a minute." He hustled over to meet her.

"What's going on?" She glanced to where Brewer and the old man waited. "You got a body or what?"

Cyrus sent an oddly covert glance in that same direction. "Before you take a look there's something you need to know."

Bree held up her hands. "Wait—have you called the lab? The coroner?" The realization that no one—*no one*—else had arrived as of yet abruptly cut through all the confusion.

Cyrus shook his head, looked at the ground before

meeting her gaze. "To tell you the truth, I didn't know who the hell to call first. This is…complicated."

"What the hell are you talking about, Cyrus?" Good grief, it wasn't like this was the first deceased victim he'd come upon.

"The vic…she's a federal agent." He scrubbed a hand over his chin.

Federal agent? "BIA?" Her first thought was that an agent from the Bureau of Indian Affairs had been murdered.

Cyrus shook his head. "FBI. Julie Grainger."

Regret hardened to a lump in Bree's gut. She'd only met Julie Grainger once. Nice lady. Young, early thirties, like Bree. A damned good agent from all indications.

"I told you this was complicated."

No kidding. "All right." Bree rubbed her forehead, an ache starting there. "I'll take a look and talk to the guide. You can call the coroner's office." *Think, Bree. This one will be sticky. Protocol has to be followed to the letter.*

"You want me to call Sheriff Martinez, too?" Cyrus suggested.

A vise clamped around Bree's chest. This was Kenner County…of course the sheriff would need to be involved. Bree heard herself say yes. What else could she say? Then she did an about-face, her movements stiff, and headed to where Brewer and the guide waited.

Patrick Martinez. Peter's father.

No matter that he had been the sheriff of the county for the last six years, somehow she had managed to avoid running into him. They hadn't spoken in nearly eight years.

Eight years!

Focus on the job.

Special Agent Julie Grainger was dead. She deserved Bree's full attention. Bree would deal with Patrick later.

* * * * *

Discover the reasons Bree Hunter kept her life-altering secret from Sheriff Patrick Martinez, and what he'll do once he finds out the truth about his son.

Bestselling author Debra Webb's
SECRETS IN FOUR CORNERS is on sale in
January 2009. One heart-stopping
KENNER COUNTY CRIME UNIT
story available every month through to September 2009!
Harlequin Intrigue is available wherever books are sold,
including most bookstores, supermarkets, discount stores
and drugstores.

REQUEST YOUR FREE BOOKS!

2 FREE NOVELS PLUS 2 FREE GIFTS!

HARLEQUIN®

INTRIGUE®

Breathtaking Romantic Suspense

YES! Please send me 2 FREE Harlequin Intrigue® novels and my 2 FREE gifts (gifts are worth about $10). After receiving them, if I don't wish to receive any more books, I can return the shipping statement marked "cancel." If I don't cancel, I will receive 6 brand-new novels every month and be billed just $4.24 per book in the U.S. or $4.99 per book in Canada. That's a savings of close to 15% off the cover price! It's quite a bargain! Shipping and handling is just 25¢ per book*. I understand that accepting the 2 free books and gifts places me under no obligation to buy anything. I can always return a shipment and cancel at any time. Even if I never buy another book from Harlequin, the two free books and gifts are mine to keep forever.

182 HDN EXGA 382 HDN EXGM

Name	(PLEASE PRINT)	

Address		Apt. #

City	State/Prov.	Zip/Postal Code

Signature (if under 18, a parent or guardian must sign)

Mail to the **Harlequin Reader Service:**
IN U.S.A.: P.O. Box 1867, Buffalo, NY 14240-1867
IN CANADA: P.O. Box 609, Fort Erie, Ontario L2A 5X3

Not valid to current subscribers of Harlequin Intrigue books.

Are you a current subscriber of Harlequin Intrigue books and want to receive the larger-print edition? Call 1-800-873-8635 today!

* Terms and prices subject to change without notice. Prices do not include applicable taxes. Sales tax applicable in N.Y. Canadian residents will be charged applicable provincial taxes and GST. Offer not valid in Quebec. This offer is limited to one order per household. All orders subject to approval. Credit or debit balances in a customer's account(s) may be offset by any other outstanding balance owed by or to the customer. Please allow 4 to 6 weeks for delivery. Offer available while quantities last.

Your Privacy: Harlequin is committed to protecting your privacy. Our Privacy Policy is available online at www.eHarlequin.com or upon request from the Reader Service. From time to time we make our lists of customers available to reputable third parties who may have a product or service of interest to you. If you would prefer we not share your name and address, please check here. ☐

HI092

Discover the
Harlequin® Romance novel
that's just right for you.

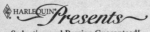

You're invited to join our Tell Harlequin Reader Panel!

By joining our new reader panel you will:

- Receive Harlequin® books—they are FREE and yours to keep with no obligation to purchase anything!
- Participate in fun online surveys
- Exchange opinions and ideas with women just like you
- Have a say in our new book ideas and help us publish the best in women's fiction

In addition, you will have a chance to win great prizes and receive special gifts!
See Web site for details. Some conditions apply.
Space is limited.

To join, visit us at
www.TellHarlequin.com.